11.25

Francis Louis Guy Smith

Winds of Ah-Mah-Ree-Yuh

A time to live, and a time to die...

Francis Louis Guy Smith

Winds of Ar-mah-Ree-yuh
Copyright © 2012 by Booksbyguy
All rights reserved. No part of this book may be reproduced or
transmitted in any form or by any means without written
permission from the author.
ISBN: 1468196073

Winds of Ar-Mah-Ree-Yuh

Dedication
To all the teenagers in our great country who have lost touch with the legacy of the west and its historical value.

Acknowledgements

All scripture and excerpts are taken from the New American Standard version of the Holy Bible. I don't think the Lord will mind. All other references are taken from Wikipedia, the free on line encyclopedia.

CHAPTER ONE

But a Samaritan, who was on a journey, came upon him; and when he saw him, he felt compassion, and came to him and bandaged up his wounds, pouring oil and wine on them; and he put him on his own beast, and brought him to an inn and took care of him. Luke 10: 33, 34

Someone he did not see had beaten him into unconsciousness. Now, he found himself bound hand and foot and dropped into a heap onto the hard packed Texas caliche. There was a blindfold covering his eyes, preventing him from seeing his assailants. Muffled voices told him his captors were nearby and he tweaked his ears trying to hear the conversation. He could only make out the smell and crackling of a fire. He was familiar with the odors of burning mesquite and the foul aroma of crackling, stinking cow chips. Twisting his wrists, he tried to free them from the hemp that was cutting off the circulation to his hands.

The posse that rode with him was bound, as was he, or had been killed by the gang of outlaws they had been trailing.

Jonah Caleb Smith had been a United States Marshall for twelve years now. He had kept the peace as well as possible in the vast territory that was Central and West Texas.

Along with twelve other men, he had trailed a band of men that had brazenly robbed the bank in Bandera in broad open daylight, shooting two men in cold blood as they galloped down the dusty street and out of town.

When the robbery happened, Jonah had been on the trail of another man who had shot one of his deputies. The deputy was trying to break up a fight in the saloon and was ambushed. The Marshall was sure that the death of his deputy had occurred to get him out of town so the outlaws could ride in and rob the bank.

Why had they not killed him? Who are these men?

He heard louder talking and arguing and tried to hear what they were saying. They were too far away and talking in low, muffled tones for him to make out their words. Shortly after the yelling had stopped and the voices had quieted, someone yanked him to his feet. He could smell the foul odor of whiskey and stale cigar smoke as he was hefted onto the back of a nervous horse. The sound of many horses riding away was confusing to him. After the sound of hooves had moved out of hearing, someone slapped his horse on the haunches and it took off at a fast gallop. Jonah had to clamp his knees onto the sides of the animal and hold on as tight as he possible could. It was a difficult thing to do with his hands still bound behind him. He swayed from side to side with the movement of the horse as it thundered across the rough terrain, not knowing where he was headed. He tried to put his feet into the stirrups but was unable to accomplish it.

The horse ran for a while, then tired, and slowed to a measured walk, snorting and sucking air into its lungs. Jonah leaned forward over the pommel and struggled to catch his breath. He had no idea where he was, or who, or why they had turned him loose. The blindfold over his eyes prevented him from getting his bearings. It seemed as if he had ridden along for hours, when his horse stumbled, whinnied loudly, and then reared, dumping him off the saddle and on to a hard rocky ground. His right ear slammed against a rock and created a severe, throbbing pain through his head. Jonah heard his horse rear several times and then gallop away, hoof beats fading in the distance, as he tried to regain his breath from the fall. He rolled to one side, feeling for a sharp edged rock, like the one he had fallen against, to cut his hands loose.

The distinct sound of a sidewinder's rattle got his attention. He stopped his motion and tried to lie very still. That sound came again, this time even closer to his face. Perspiration was streaming down his face and he ceased the rubbing action to loosen his hands.

The loud, sharp crack of a rifle caused him to jump and then recoil away from the direction where he thought the snake was. Fragment of chipped rock cut into his face from a bullet ricocheting. The next sound was the double click of a Henry lever, opening and closing to put another cartridge into an empty chamber.

"You dang near got snake bit partner." A voice spoke to him. "Shore looks like you got yoreself in a fix"

"I guess I did. Think you can untie my hands?" Jonah had not a clue who was talking to him.

"I spect I can do that."

Jonah felt the pull of a blade on the hemp that held his wrist together, and then his hands dropped limply to his sides. He slowly lifted his tingling fingers to the blindfold and removed it from his eyes.

"I owe you my life Mister, you got a name?" He blinked in the bright sunlight trying to focus on who his benefactor was.

"Names don't mean a whole bunch out here. Just be glad I come along. That sidewinder was just about to give you some hurt."

"Where's my horse? Did you see him?"

"Yep. He run off away. I'll go see if I can fetch him while you skin that sidewinder. No need him goin to waste. You got somethin to build a fire with?" The stranger got up and walked to his own horse.

Jonah pulled the knife from his scabbard, and proceeded to skin the snake, then gathered up mesquite twigs to start a small fire. He had just gotten a flame started when the stranger rode up, leading his mount behind him. He was happy to see the animal. It would have been a long walk to somewhere after he found which way to go.

"You a lawman?" The stranger looked at him curiously.

"How did you know?" Jonah looked back with the same curious gaze. He felt his chest and found his badge no longer there.

"That cayuse looks like a lawman's horse, that and that federal brand." All Marshall's rode animals provided by the U.S. government.

They sat in silence and ate the roasted meat. The old man that had saved Jonah's life, stood and wiped his hands on his pants and simply said,

"Later friend". He mounted his horse and rode away to the west, leaving Jonah to wonder who he was.

The sun was beginning to settle over the western skyline. The Marshall got his bedroll from a tired horse, found a place against a boulder, and settled down for the night. He did not know why or what had transpired that day, but he would have to get back to Bandera to start a trail.

---------- ….. ----------

He rode into town amidst a clamor of activity. The bank manager, who was also the bank owner, almost beat Jonah to his desk.

"Where you been Marshall? Them deputies, that ain't dead, come back to town three days ago. You find them robbers."

"I've been kinda tied up Mister Stephens. I'll let you know when I find them robbers…..and your money." Jonah was somewhat irritated at the man who had sat behind a desk in his own comfortable office while he nearly lost his life trying to recover the bank's money. He was still confused as to why the outlaws had turned him loose.

Stephens stormed out of the Marshall's office and across the street to his bank.

It would be hard for Jonah to find enough men in Bandera to form another posse. The whole town knew how many of them had been ambushed and killed by the gang of outlaws.

Jonah washed his hands in the basin and gently wiped at the dried blood on the side of his face, from his encounter with a hard rock. He strolled down the boardwalk to the café and ordered himself a big steak dinner, with a whole pot of strong, black coffee. Sitting alone in a corner, he felt the eyes of everyone in the room sneaking glances at him.

After he had eaten a good steak, he went through his normal walk through of the town, checking doors and looking through windows, terminating at the small rooming house that he called home. It was time for him to fall into a real bed for a good night's sleep. He knew he would not get back there for a long while.

Jonah was up and out before daylight and rode out of town alone, once more on the trail of outlaws. Turning to the northwest, he headed for the last place he knew the outlaws to be, the place where they had, for some unknown reason, turned him loose.

Jonah backtracked from where the man had shot the snake and cut him loose from his predicament He found the tracks of his horse and followed them to where they had started his blindfolded ride. He dismounted and walked the area over looking for some sign of where the robbers had gone. Following the multitude of riders for a ways to the southeast, he came to a point where the tracks simply stopped. He circled around for a while and found that the owl hoots had brushed away their tracks. They had taken great pains to cover up their trail, and had done a good job of it. Jonah rode around for two hours and never did locate the trail again. He continued on to the southeast, the direction they started out.

Riding until the sun was too low to provide light, he stopped and built a fire and made a pot of coffee. He removed the New Testament from his saddlebags. It was the one that he had carried with him since the Great War in the South. Settling down with a hot cup, he scanned the Word for some verse that would ease his mind and give him direction as he always had in these circumstances.

When he woke, there was a visitor across the fire from his bedroll. He was squatted on his haunches waiting for the Marshall to wake. Jonah recognized him right away, although it had been years since they had seen each other. He was a Tonkawa Indian brave called Iron Wolf. He was one of the Tonkawa who had cut Jonah loose from where Apaches had staked him out in the sun to die.

"Iron Wolf my friend. It has been many moons." Jonah spoke softly to his friend.'

"Many moons. You still man of the white man law?" Iron Wolf remembered what Jonah had become.

"Yes, I still track the bad man. Have you seen the bad man?"

"See much bad man. See bad man all time." He waved his arm in a circle encompassing the whole landscape. "See bad man you look for, ride to big town, where Mission called Al a mo. They not ride in together, ride in two by two."

"Thanks Iron Wolf. I go see Alamo Town." Jonah saddled his horse, and waived to Iron Wolf as he rode slowly toward San Antonio, leaving the Indian still squatted on his haunches.

After a few minutes, he turned in his saddle to see Iron Wolf loping off to the southwest toward his village near the Big Bend. It was nice to see an old friend again.

The Tonkawa had been a friend and ally since Jonah came to Texas after the civil war. He wondered about all the friends that had made the journey with him. He had seen the Browns, the freed slaves, who had become ranch owners. In his travels in the duties of a Marshall, he stopped by to visit them when he was up their way in Loraine, Texas.

Benjamin Stark stopped by occasionally to visit him in Bandera between trail drives, as did Abe Tobias. Abe had started out when he arrived in Texas, to be a newspaper printer, but gave it up to answer the call of the cattle drive. Sometimes he and Ben Stark drove together and sometimes went their separate ways, depending on which way the wind called them. He had not seen the mountain man, of the group, Samson Raines, since he took off for the Colorado Territory some twelve years ago. Samson Raines had married a Tonkawa maiden and taken her with him to the high country. That was the talk anyway,

Jonah caught himself day dreaming and knew his mind must get back to the business at hand. The business of tracking down a bunch of bank robbers and seeing they paid for killing his deputy and the other two townspeople.

Somewhere in the home of the Alamo were six or eight men who had committed the crime. He did not know the exact number, but eventually would find out and put them in jail, if they did not resist. Jonah was a Marshall who tried to bring everyone in alive. It was against his belief to take a life and he only did so if he was pushed into it.

He rode into the town feeling as if everyone was watching him. A feeling he very seldom got. Jonah watched and waited for the next two days, looking for some sign that the culprits were spending money that was not their own. After finding nothing in San Antonio, he headed back to Bandera to face the bank man, Ed Stephens. He didn't relish the chore.

Chapter Two

He executes justice for the orphan and the widow, and shows his love for the alien by giving him food and clothing.
Deuteronomy 10:18

Abraham Ezekiel Tobias walked into a stage station in Abilene, Kansas. He had just finished a trail drive with Jesse Chisholm and had two month's pay in his pocket. He had been thinking about his youth on this whole drive. Abraham did not know who his parents were. He had been dropped off and raised from birth until he was sold, in an orphanage in Newark, New Jersey.

On this drive, he had developed a strong yearning to go back to his roots. He had joined the union army at sixteen as one of the elite Fifth New York Volunteer Infantry. They wore colorful uniforms like the French Army.

———————— ….. ————————

Before joining the army Abe had run away from a man who was a severe taskmaster, using him as a slave to plow during the day and working him to the point of sheer exhaustion at night, mucking out stalls and feeding the stock. The man had a dislike for the Jewish community and was taking his hatred out on the young boy in his care.

A farmer, he had two sons of his own, who were extremely lazy and not compelled to do the chores that Abe could do. He had taken the young Jewish lad from the orphanage that did not provide a place for displaced children.

The old woman, who took them in for a fee, farmed them out for another donation as apprentices or laborers. The Hebrew Benevolent Society was poor and had more children than they could handle, so they passed them out at very young age.

Abe had run away from the farm at twelve and made his way to the big city of New York. There, he hoped to get lost in the crowds of people and find a place to call home. For months, he had fed himself from trashcans, or on whatever morsels of food he could wrestle from one of the other children who were competing for what scraps they could find.

There were many nights of sleeping with an empty stomach and wishing for the food he had been given by the angry taskmaster's wife back on the farm. He, like many of the other waifs, cried himself to sleep many night.

On one of those forages for food, he noticed a man watching him from the back doorway of a print shop. He brazenly stepped up to the man.

"You got any work to be done mister? I'm a hard worker." His voice was pleading for help. "I'll work for food."

"Who is there Augustus?" The voice came from somewhere inside the room behind the man.

"It is just a boy, Mama. He needs some food Mama. We have some gnashes for a hungry boy?"

"We got no food. Send him away" The woman had seen others begging for food on the streets of New York. She came to the door to send him away. She looked down at the young boy standing at her door. "Oh, such beautiful big brown eyes. Papa, I get this boy some gnashes. You wait!" She directed her last comment to the brown-eyed youngster standing at her stoop.

"The man was Augustus Bromfield, and he was looking for a printer's apprentice to help him through the long days of bending backbreaking work of setting type. He was getting old and the work was becoming increasingly harder for him.

"Mama, I think we make this one a printer. What you think, Mama?"

I think he has such beautiful brown eyes like you Papa. I think we feed this boy."

Until the civil war called to him at sixteen, Abe spent his days in the print shop of Augustus Bromfield. learning the trade of a print setter, he became very good and very fast.

After work, which was sometime late into the night, he roamed the street and played with some of the youngsters he used to fight for food. When he could, he slipped them bits of food.

When the civil war started, Abe, like so many other young boys, was pressed into the service of his country. Many times, he contemplated changing his mind and running away again, but when the coach pulled in he took a deep breath, boarded with many other young men, and rode off to war. The uniforms of the Fifth New York Volunteer Infantry were colorful and flamboyant, and enticed many youngsters into becoming soldiers.

For four long years, Abe fought alongside of, and watched many children lose their life. He spent many nights with his head buried in the ground, suffering from the same kind of hunger he did on a New Jersey farm, and on the streets of New York

In a South Mississippi swamp at the end of the war, he found a God he had not been told about in the Orthodox Jewish family of Augustus Bromfield. He found him when he was all alone, hungry, cold and wet, with one of the only possession he had left. He read the New Testament Bible he had been given as a new recruit at the beginning of the war. The only other possession was a knife, a tool for taking lives. He had vowed never to use it for that again.

While he was praying for a way out of his circumstances, he had heard the sound of someone walking along the river's edge.

It initiated him on an odyssey to Texas, the Promised Land, with three new friends.

_____ ….. _____

Abe walked out of the stage station in Abilene with a ticket in his hand. His destination was New York, city. He sat on a bench and waited the hour for the stage to arrive.

A journey had begun that would take him back to a place he had been running from for a long, long time. He wondered about the Bromfield's who he had not seen for more than six years.

After two long weeks of bumpy riding, waiting for connecting stage lines, and conversations with people he would never see again, the coach finally arrived in the big city. He stepped down from the coach and walked into a crowd of bustling, rushing people. All of them seemed to be in a hurry to get somewhere.

Things had changed since Abe had last seen the big city. The war had been over for more than two years now and some of those who had made money from the killing of their fellow men were trying hard to take what they could from the living.

None of the streets looked as they had when he marched away with a proud army troop.

He walked down the streets trying to find where the Bromfield print shop was. He gazed at street sign looking for one that said forty fifth. When he finally found it, he strolled along slowly watching the people scurrying by. The injured and dismembered men seated on the sidewalks begging for handouts saddened him.

After a while, some things, like door stoops, began to look familiar to him, and he found himself standing in front of a brownstone building. It was no longer a print shop, but a very busy butcher shop... He walked in off the street and tried to remember what it was like when he left. The smell of printers ink had been replaced by the odor of decayed meat.

"This used to be the Bromfield print shop." He spoke to a man wearing a white apron.

"It is butcher shop. I don't know from the printing. You want to buy some meat. If no, get out of the way of my customer. They buy the meat! Good meat. Steak comes all the way from Texas. You know Texas meat. Is good?"

Abe walked back out onto the busy sidewalk. He turned to walk the two blocks to the building where the Bromfield's had lived in a small downstairs apartment. The doors and windows were boarded over.

There was no sign that the Bromfield's or the shop where he had learned to print, had ever existed. It was a sad moment for Abe.

He found a small cheap hotel room and then walked up and down the streets, under the lights, amazed at all the nighttime activity that was taking place. There were girls in skimpy outfits peering out of doors and windows, trying to lure men in. Player pianos banged into the cool night air. To him, the laughter was out of place with so many wounded veterans. It was much different from when he had spent a childhood on these streets.

He found a steak and a cup of coffee at one of the sidewalk cafes and turned back to his hotel for an early bed. His thoughts went to a cup of coffee while seated around a fire on a cattle drive.

Abe woke to a much quieter morning with virtually no one on the sidewalks except an occasional man pushing a broom. He ambled down the way for fifteen blocks and found where he had gotten off the stage. There was a lone figure sweeping the trash from the night before. "Where can I get a stage to Newark?" he asked the sweeper.

"Ain't no stage to Newark! One of them weird things they call Caps carriages or something like that, goes over there. Ought to be one by here in a little while. Look for one of them kinda yellow rigs with a canvas top."

Sure enough, in thirty minutes, a long yellow carriage stopped at the curb and the driver yelled.

"All aboard for Newark, New Jersey. Going to Jersey, Mister? Get on while I go get me a cup of coffee."

When Abe opened the door, he saw two long seats inside. Unlike stagecoaches, the seats ran from front to back. He was the only passenger.

An hour later the carriage found the Newark Benevolent Society address and dropped Abe in front.

The doors were much smaller than he remembered as a boy. He walked up the steps, found a worn doorknocker, and knocked violently.

He remembered as a youngster, waiting and sleeping in the hallway for someone to pick him up and give him a home. When the door had opened, a farmer took him by the arm and dragged him to a waiting wagon.

He knocked again and an elderly Jewish woman greeted his knock. The same woman had given him to the farmer.

"Mrs. Goldstein?"

"Yes, may I help you? Are you looking for a child to adopt?" She tried to force a smile. We only have one boy, but I'm sure he'll work out fine."

"No, I just wanted to see if you were as ugly and mean looking as I remember."

"I beg your pardon! The old woman lost her fake smile. "Who are you?" She became indignant.

"I'm one of the boys you gave to a farmer to use as a slave. I survived. Many didn't. I am here to see that you lose your job, Mrs. Goldstein! If you chose to quit, I won't tell the law about you. If you don't, I will have you and that weasel you call a husband arrested."

The look on the woman's face turned to fear. "Well, I am going to retire from this job anyway. I don't need this kind of tomfoolery."

She tried to close the door, but Abe stuck his foot into the opening. "I will be back next week. See that you are gone before then" He turned and walked slowly away, not looking back

Abe walked along the street thinking about the many boys who had been mistreated by the orphanage, and how many lost their lives in a war that made no sense and resolved nothing.

He found a stagecoach station and mounted a hard leather seat for another long ride. This one would be going to the Promised Land called Texas and the service of his Lord.

Chapter Three

Woe to you, scribes and Pharisees, hypocrites! For you clean the outside of the cup and of the dish, but inside they are full of robbery and self- indulgence. Matthew 23:25

When Jonah tied his horse at the hitching rail in front of his office, he noticed two others there. He guessed someone was waiting to talk to him about a bank robbery. He dismounted and thoughtfully wondered who it could be this time. Slowly, and feeling the heaviness of his job for the first time, he climbed the steps to the boardwalk. He opened the door and walked across the threshold very cautiously.

There were two men waiting for him inside. One of them had taken a seat at his chair behind the old pine desk and the other was lying on a cell bunk pretending to sleep. The one behind his desk was a face he did not know. The other, in the cell, he could not see under the hat that covered his face.

"Can I help you with something?" He addressed the unknown face seated at his desk, while warily, watching the other man out of the corner of his eye.

"You could pour an old friend a cup of coffee." It was the prone one in the cell speaking. He sat up and removed his hat. It was Ben Stark. "How you doing lawman?'

"Howdy, Ben. Who's that sitting in a tired man's chair?"

"This is Johnny Warren. I picked him up in the Texas panhandle. We been driving cows together."

"Howdy Marshall, Ben's told me a lot about you."

"Mostly lies I'll wager." Jonah was glad to see Ben, but the pressure of what was going on was obvious on his face.

"Got problems, Jonah?"

"Some. I could use a couple of deputies. Know where I can find any?"

"I haven't been a lawman since we run off and shot all them rustlers, that was trying to steal Moses and Aaron Brown's herd. How long has that been? Twelve years I reckon."

"How about your partner? He ever been on the right side of the law?" Jonah looked at Johnny.

"He got on the right side of the Lord back in Santa Fe. Does that count?" Ben smiled at Jonah, already knowing the answer.

"I guess he'll do. Does he know how to shoot, just in case we have to?" Jonah knew that Ben knew he only did that as a last resort. He wanted Johnny to know that too.

"Johnny, you ought to know that Jonah brings all them outlaws in alive. Least ways as many as he can, so don't go round shooting everybody." Ben looked at Johnny more serious than ever...

"Where do we start looking?" Ben asked

"I'm not sure. They just seem to have disappeared. This is kind of a peculiar case." Jonah proceeded to tell his two new deputies all the details, from his deputy getting shot, to the outlaws not killing him. There seemed to be more questions than answers.

"I'm no lawman but, it sounds like somebody in town here knew what was happening. Somebody knew how to get you out of town." It was the young man Johnny Warren expressing what Jonah had already suspected.

"I think we might make a lawman out of this youngster." Jonah laughed. "I think we will go back to San Antonio. I must have missed something there. Or… Better yet, I'll check around some of the outlying towns, while you two hang around town for a day or two. Nobody will pay any mind to a couple of cow chasers waiting for their next herd."

"Sounds like a good plan." Ben injected.

"Keep your badges out of sight. We'll leave town separate. You go first, heading to San Antone.

Jonah rode out toward San Antonio and when he was a good distance out of Bandera, turned to the southwest, to throw a wide loop around the area where he had been tracking the robbers. He rode the rest of that day in a wide circle looking for tracks or sign. He could find no evidence of a large bunch of riders.

After two days of futile searching, he turned his trail to Las Gallinas to wait for Ben and Johnny, wondering if they had turned up anything in San Antonio. He camped on the edge of the sweet water creek that ran through and carried the same name as the small settlement of Las Gallinas. There were five structures in what the Mexicans who lived there called a Colonia. One of them was a cantina that was owned and hosted by a large bodied, loud old Mexican woman, who shook all over when she laughed. She would let anyone hang around her place as long as they treated her girl's right. They were three younger, but well versed, ladies' in the wiles of Mama Magdalene's business.

Mama knew Jonah well from his many adventures of trailing outlaws through her establishment. He had even arrested a couple much to her displeasure. Outlaws knew there was a safe haven as long as they caused no disturbance, or brought attention, to lawmen like Marshall Jonah Smith.

When Jonah walked through the hanging beaded entry, a quiet hush fell on the place. He looked around and found Mama Magdalene seated at a table with two of her girls counting Pesos they had turned over to her.

She saw him come in and quickly dropping the dinero into her pocket shooed the girls away. Jonah strolled across the room and seated himself at the table with the immense proprietor.

"Howdy Mama. How's business?"

"It was better till you show up." She snarled at him.

"I don't want to bother you Mama, I'm looking for a bunch of galoots who robbed a bank over at Bandera. Heard anything?"

"If I hear, I no tell you! You law dog, bad for business. Why you no come back no more? Make Mama happy!"

"I tracked some horses to your back door." He lied to her to see her reaction.

She turned and looked to the back room. She shouted. "Anybody sees a bunch of Cayuse with gringos carry mucho dinero? I think not. Now you leave, so my customer's spend many pesos."

Jonah walked slowly to the doorway scanning the room. A couple of hombres lowered their heads under sombreros as he passed by.

He threw a leg over the saddle and rode to the edge of town, to a place on the creek where he could still see the cantina. It was getting dusk so he built a small fire and sat a blue pot filled with water to one side to boil for coffee. He read his New Testament in the glow of the flames while he had his coffee. Listening to the raucous laughter and tambourine music from Mama Magdalene's, he finally dozed off to sleep.

The familiar sound of the double click from a Henry lever action forty caliber snapped his eyes open and he rolled to one side, not knowing where the sound had come from. He rolled just in time to hear the crack of a rifle and see the dust fly from his bedroll where he had been only a moment before. He rolled again and found the backside of a pinion tree to block the shots that were being fired at him. Bullets ricocheted off the tree splintering the bark and he scrunched down and quickly dragged his saddle in front of him to provide some more protection. He couldn't see who was firing at him, but there was more than one.

    A sudden volley of shots splattered dust all around him, and he knew he would have to find a safer place than this if he were to survive. Jonah crawled quickly toward the creek with bullets spraying all around him. He was on the creek bank when he heard a round of shots coming from a different direction. They were directed at the men who had been firing at him. He lowered his head and caught his breath, then managed to pull his six-gun and begin to help return the fire as he scrambled up the creek bank.

    He heard the sound of horse's hooves as several men mounted and started away and then suddenly stopped.

    Johnny Warren rode into his gun-riddled camp and dismounted, six-gun still in his hands. "Them hombres got something against you Marshall?" Johnny asked and then smiled. "I didn't know if them was the ones you take alive or the ones you shoot, so we just scared em a little. You know who they are."

"I don't know, but I suspect they were bank robbers." Jonah answered. "You boys find anything in Alamo town?"

"Word is, there was somebody about to get audited, and couldn't make muster. Must of thought you found something. Oh by the by, we hired on you another deputy while we was in town. He's gone to help Ben round up them friends of yours"

Jonah looked at him. "And…?"

"Cow herder by the name of Tobias, Abe Tobias. Ever hear of him?"

Jonah got a big smile on his face. "Seems like I heard that name before. I guess we'll take him on." Abe Tobias was one of the four that came to Texas at the end of the civil war. Jonah had not seen their friend in more than a year.

"I guess we better go help them round up them owl hoots. The two of them mounted and rode to where Ben and Abe had ambushed the six men who had been shooting at Jonah.

When they found Ben and Abe with the bandits in tow, Jonah welcomed Abe, and thanked him for the help. "All we need now is old Samson and the Browns." It had been more than twelve years since Jonah, Ben, or Abe had seen Samson. They missed their old friend.

Johnny had heard some of the names and had met Abe in San Antonio with Ben.

After depositing the robbers in the jail in San Antonio, the four of them rode to Bandera. They devised a plan along the way to try to trap Ed Stephens into showing his hand, if he was involved in the robbery and they knew he was. His friends had told them so.

Jonah rode slowly and alone into town while Ben, Abe, and Johnny circled around and came in on a back street that would bring them to the back door of the bank.

Jonah dismounted at his office and very deliberately climbed the steps. He stopped on the boardwalk, and turned and stared at the front of the bank for several minutes. He removed his revolver and spun the cylinder to check for cartridges then looked toward the bank again. He walked into his office, stayed only a moment, and stepped back onto the walk. He looked both ways up and down the street and then back at the bank as if he were contemplating something. Finally, he checked his revolver again, holstered it and stepped decisively down into the street and started across.

As he approached the bank, Ben, Abe, and Johnny walked from around the side of the building escorting Ed Stephens. Ben was carrying a satchel filled with greenbacks and gold coins "I think your banker was getting ready to take a trip. Had a horse tied out back, just waiting?" Johnny grinned.

Were you going somewhere Mister Stephens? The owl hoots you sent after me decided to tell a story about you and your robbery." Jonah grabbed him by the arm and walked across the street bringing the banker to the jail cell in the back of his office. When he had locked the man in, he stepped out into the office where the three cowhands waited.

"What are you three going to do now?"' Jonah looked at them seriously.

"I guess we'll go find some cows to punch. Our work here is done!" Johnny played it like a stage play drama, and dropped his badge on the Marshall's desk.

Ben dropped his too. Abe shook his shoulders. He didn't have a badge.

Surprising the other three, Jonah removed the badge from his chest and dropped it with the others. They stared at him, waiting.

"I'm done being a lawman. I'm going to do something I've thought about for a long, long time. Twelve years long! Now I am going to do what I was picked to do by the Lord. I am going to spread the Gospel to whoever will listen."

His friends stared at him for a moment. All of them had had the same call in their lives. Even the Jewish boy from New York who had met the Lord on a civil war battlefield in Mississippi. They walked out into a new wind and a fresh start in the lives of all four.

Chapter Four

After Job opened his mouth and cursed the day of his birth. And Job said, Let the day perish on which I was to be born, And the night which said, A boy is conceived. Job 3:1-3

Ryan Hale woke to a beautiful early fall morning in Santa Fe, New Mexico. It could not have been a happier time for the new young man of God. He had become an ordained minister of the Word of God. Ordained in his own father's church. Or, at least the only father he had known since the age of twelve, when he and his sister Melissa had been rescued from an Apache war party. Joseph McKinley and his wife Ruth, had adopted the two children, but had insisted they keep the name of their true father.

Ryan was married to Maria, A young Mexican and Navajo maiden that he and two friends had saved from a blowing Arizona snowstorm.

Ryan and Maria had taken the vows of wedlock in Joseph McKinley's church in Santa Fe, New Mexico on a cold January morning shortly after he had returned home from the search for a man that had sent him to prison. Jose Gonzales had returned to Santa Fe and told the truth that set Ryan free from a murder that he had not committed.

Now on this cool September morn, Ryan was looking forward to moving to Lincoln County, to assume the role of Pastor in a small rural setting.

He and his wife Maria were expecting the arrival of their first child and had the permission of their small new congregation to wait until the baby was born to move to their church. Ryan was excited about the prospect of becoming a father. He would guard this child with his life as his father had done for him and his sister.

His sister Melissa or "Sissy" as he had always addressed her was coming today to be with Maria. Ruth, the Reverend's wife was there to help and according to her calculation, this was to be the day.

Ryan sat on the back porch of the small home of his stepparents awaiting Sissy's arrival. He was enjoying a hot black cup of coffee from his mother's wood stove.

As he was deep in thought, a shrill scream pierced the early morning quiet. It took him a moment to gather himself, and then the scream came again. It was his wife Maria. She was yelling out his name.

"Oh, my Lord. It is time and Sissy's not here yet." He blurted the words out loud.

Ryan was beside himself as he looked down the road for a buggy, and rushed through the kitchen door. Ruth was already on her way to the small room that Ryan and Maria had shared since their wedding day. Maria was screaming even louder now.

Then there was a silence that shook him to his knees. The slap of a hand on its rear brought forth a loud cry from a baby child. Ryan felt a sense of relief at the sound of his first-born. He stood anxiously outside the door as his father came into the room from somewhere outside with a large smile on his face.

The door opened softly and Ruth stepped into the room holding an infant wrapped in a white parcel of cloth. "Meet you son, Ryan." She spoke with a shiver in her voice.

A door opened and Sissy called out "Hello. I'm here. Is it time yet?" She stopped when she saw Ruth holding the child. "It's already here!" She squealed and rushed to the side of her brother and his new baby. "Maria did a great job. She gave you a boy! How is Maria?"

In the excitement of his son, Ryan had not asked.

"Maria did not make it!" The sound of those words sent shocks up the spine of the young minister. His hand stopped halfway to his son and looked at his mother's face where tears were streaming down.

"What! No! She's alright! She has to be! She is my wife! God would not do this to me! Please God! We must wake her up! Papa, Ma! We must wake her up. She's just sleeping from the baby! God! I am your son! I am a minister of your Word. Why would you do this to me?" Ryan fell to his knee's weeping and holding his face in his hands. He crawled through the bedroom door and across to where his wife lay peacefully.

Sissy followed slowly behind him. Tears streamed down her face too. "She in a better place now Ryan." She realized as the words came out that they were not what her brother wanted to hear.

Ryan had taken care of her since they were children and now she could not think of a way to help him in his grief.

Ryan rose slowly to his feet and looked at his sister with a blank stare. He turned his gaze upward and Sissy saw a look on her brother's face like she had never seen before. It was a near satanic look of hatred. "You can have my wife God, but you can't have me. I will never praise your name again. I want nothing to do with you." He stared at the ceiling and yelled at the top of his lungs. "You hear me God. I will never speak to you again! You leave me alone! I don't belong to you!" Ryan turned and without even looking at his newborn son stormed out of the house.

_____ ..... _____

Jose Gonzales was sweeping out the church for the Reverend in preparation for next Sunday. It was to be a very special service this week. Young Ryan who was now a minister was going to help christen his own child that would come into the world sometime this week.

A loud scream shrieked through the morning air and Jose stopped his sweeping and listened to see what it was and where it had come from. It came again. This time it sounded like a woman was calling to his friend Ryan. It sounded like Maria, the young wife of his friend.

Jose dropped the broom and walked to the back door of the Reverends home and listened to hear what was happening.

For a short time, there was silence, then they heard the bellowing of his friend Ryan. Then the hard slam of the front door of the house. Then, the silence once more. Jose treaded softly to the kitchen door and rapped very lightly on the door facing. Senora Ruth came to see who was there. She told Jose to come in, then, called to her husband. "Joseph, Jose is here. Will you see him?" She seemed to be in shock and not sure what to say to the Mexican man who was at her door.

Ryan Hale had spent two years in Yuma Territorial prison because Jose had given false testimony at his trial. Ryan had searched for Jose for months trying to clear his name, after being, inadvertently, released from prison. Ryan never found Jose, but the Mexican had showed up at the Reverends doorstep and told all, to clear Ryan from the crime he had not committed.

Jose had been a barroom drunk, who would do anything for a drink and had been coerced into lying to frame Ryan by a group of ranchers involved in the

Lincoln County Wars. The day Jose showed up in Santa Fe he had found the Lord, and over time, he and Ryan had become friends.

——————— ..... ———————

Ryan staggered down the street to Ivan's livery stable and with blinding tears flowing from his eyes, mounted a horse, and rode at a full gallop out of Santa Fe. Not once did he look back or think about the son he was leaving behind. He did not even give him a name. He let the horse have his head after pointing him eastward toward Texas and out of New Mexico. Vowing never to come back or speak the name of God again.

The horse he was riding began to labor in its breathing, but this time Ryan did not care. Once before he had ridden a horse beyond its limits, and that time he had stopped and thanked the Lord for saving the two of them. He had even given that horse a name. He had called it Abraham, a faithful servant of the Lord. This time that would not happen.

He rode on and on into the desert land of New Mexico, wanting to die while he cursed the Lord. Somewhere in the late afternoon, the horse stumbled and went down, dumping Ryan onto the hard caliche and gravel desert floor.

The horse rolled over and tried to get to his feet, but the strength had been sapped from his body and he was unable to rise. Ryan lay on the hard pan and continued to cry. He had lost the one thing that he thought the Lord had given him for life. Now she was gone forever. He had nothing to live for and just didn't care anymore.

"Take me Lord! You don't care about me. Why did you take my Maria!? Why did you take my life! She was my love! She loved you with all her heart! Why!? Why!?" Ryan sobbed till there was no more in him to release, then he went silent. He rolled and looked at the horse that had also gone silent. The horse had done what Ryan wanted to do at that moment. The horse had breathed its last breath while Ryan cursed God and felt sorry for himself.

Ryan Hale lay broken and sobbing on a desert floor until he had no more and then he fell asleep.

He woke to a cool autumn morning that felt cold to him. He stumbled to his feet and staggered into a rising sun, determined to make it to Texas if God didn't take him first. He had no food or water to help him sustain life, but he did not care. Staggering sideways at times, he continued to shake his fist at the sky and curse the Lord. For two days, he hobbled along into the dry land until he was beginning to see food on a table before his eyes. He saw a running stream of water, cold and clear only fifty yards away. He lurched forward and the stream moved fifty yards farther away.

Clambering to his feet again, he tried to run so the stream could not get away from him before he got to it. Again, when he fell to his knees at the waters' edge it was gone. He was becoming delirious. He did not care. He cursed at the heavens again. "Take me! Come on! Take me! I don't care! Take me!"

He fell to a prone position and buried his face in his hands, and once again began to sob uncontrollably.

Ryan rambled alone through the flat land talking to himself and cursing God with virtually every breath. He fell again and tried to crawl. He heard the sound of a sidewinder rattling close by... "Here you go! Here's your chance! You can get me right here, Right now. Come on! Do it!" He shook his fist into the air another time. Ryan felt his breath ebbing away and knew that God was finally going to do what he had been begging him to do. The last sound he heard was the crack of a rifle that silenced the sidewinder's rattle.

Chapter Five

Pursue peace with all men, and the sanctification without which no one will see the Lord. See to it that no one comes short of the grace of God; that no root of bitterness springing up causes trouble, and by it many be defiled; Hebrews 12:14,15

Jose Gonzales took a canvas bag from Ruth McKinley and tied it carefully onto the saddle behind where he would sit. He stepped tentavely into the stirrup and slung his right leg over. He barely heard the words that were being spoken to him.

It had been a year since Jose had had a drink, and he thanked the Lord for that. It had also been a year since he had wandered the land trying to stay one-step ahead of Ryan and the other men who were after him. Those other men wanted him dead. Now here he was about to embark on a trail that would find him tracking his friend to try to bring him home to his family and to his new son.

Joseph and Ruth were both speaking directions to him at the same time. Melissa was standing back waiting her turn to speak. She simply said to him. "Please Jose, find my brother."

He rode off in the direction that the liveryman, Ivan, said that Ryan had gone. He rode slow, partly out of fear and partly because he vaguely remembered his last journey into the great state of Texas. It was going to be a scary trip and hopefully a short one.

———— ….. ————

Jose Juan Gonzales was born of young parents in Ciudad, Victoria, Mexico. Juan and Consuela, were peons and under the watchful control of a very cruel master. Somehow, when Jose was only two years old, they made their escape in the middle of the night. They wore only what was on their backs and made off with barely enough food to get them to the Rio Grande river.

The frightened couple, crossed the border near Matamoras, and, were making their way to freedom in a new country they had heard so much about. Juan had already made plans to find work on one of the many gringo ranches.

Two days of walking in their new found, country brought them no further to the freedom they had sought. Because they had no way of building a fire, they slept huddled together, in each other's arms, with Jose between them. Eating only the prickly pears, they found, from cactus.

One early morning Consuela opened her eyes to see seven Apache warriors standing above them watching them sleep. Her screams woke Juan and he jumped to his feet to protect his wife and child. One of the fierce, angry warriors knocked him to the ground and put a spear to his throat, subduing him. They drug the couple to a thorny tree and hung them by their thumbs. They laughed as they stuck the sharp points of spears far enough into their flesh to make them scream in pain.

One of the brutal red men tied the baby Jose's hands behind him and sat him harshly on the ground in full view of his parents. The two year old cried and watched in terror as the red devils removed the skin from his mother and father. They continued the game until both stopped screaming in pain, and had died from their torture. The Apache mounted up and rode away, laughing and pointing over their shoulder at the baby who had fallen onto his side. Jose, was left to absorb the horror in front of him, through tear distorted eyes

A band of Tonkawa Indians came by two days later and cut the boy loose, then dug shallow graves to bury the two mutilated and unrecognizable bodies.

Jose stayed with the Tonkawa until he was twelve years old, then made his way into a town, and found a bottle of whiskey would take away the frightening nightmares. He stayed that way, wondering from town to town, until someone paid him to tell a lie that would send a man to prison.

Jose was now on the trail of the man he had sent away, and then helped to release from his prison. Jose had lost the images of his mother and father sitting on the pew of Joseph McKinley's church. Now he must help his friend Ryan Hale lose his image of a dead wife

Two days out of Santa Fe, he came upon the dead carcass of the horse that Ryan had ridden into the ground. There was the sign of another man's boot prints and the head of a sidewinder stinking in the sun. It appeared someone had lifted Ryan onto another animal and carried him away. Jose was not very good at tracking, but this horse was not hard to follow.

He trailed the rider until he had lost the tracks in the descending sunlight that dropped over the horizon behind him. He built a small fire and ate the cold biscuit and ham that Ruth McKinley had given him. He was still afraid that Indians might find him and slept very little.

At first light, he found the tracks again and began slowly riding along over them being very vigilant of his surroundings. He rode that day until once again the sun sinking over the western skyline made it hard for him to see. Jose dismounted and once again partook of one of Ruth McKinley's biscuits, with only water to wash it down. A coyote howled in the distance alerting him to the possibility of Indians nearby. He had heard the Tonkawa imitate animal sounds, and knew few white men could tell the difference, including him.

Another night with no sleep made it difficult to keep his mind on the task. He would find himself dozing off and waking not knowing how far he had ridden since he last looked for tracks.

—————— ..... ——————

Ryan opened his eyes and wondered where he was. This wasn't at all what he pictured hades to be. Surely, hades didn't have the smell of a dirty barnyard. He opened his eyes a little wider and found his vision not to clear from all the sobbing he had done before he came to this place.

The surrounding became vaguely familiar but he didn't know how far he had come or where he may be. Obviously, God had not taken him as he wanted. A voice out of his past, cut through the cool morning stench of horse manure. "Mister, I don't why you come back here. Him or his Pa ain't gonna like you bein here."

Suddenly Ryan was aware of where he was. He had stopped at this tumbling down scrapyard of a place while he was trailing Jose Gonzales from Texas back into New Mexico. It was where the girl's husband had threatened to do him in for messin with his wife. This time Ryan had not ridden in looking for water. Someone had brought him here. "Where is your husband? Did he bring me here?"

"I don't know what you talkin bout. Ain't nobody brung you here! He gonna shoot you, he find you here!"

"Leave that boy alone girl! Yore husband ketch you back here he gonna switch you good." The old man who had been passed out in the front yard on Ryan's last stop, had come around the corner of the barn. "Now you be a good gal, I won't tell"

The old man turned to Ryan. "You was dang near dead out there when I come up. You was rantin and ravin at somebody. Snake was getting ready to give you what fer. He gonna be good in the pot tonight! You eat snake boy?"

"No thanks. I'm not hungry" Ryan did not care if he ever ate again.

"Suit yoreself. I'm gonna like that varmint. Gal, you go get this here one a dipper of water. Don't get too close. Last time his hands was tied but he got loose and skedaddled." The old man chuckled and walked around the barn.

Ryan thought about Maria and, what he thought God had done to him. Tears formed in the corners of his eyes again.

"What's a matter mister? That old man hurt you?"

Ryan did not respond. No one could ever hurt him again. He would never ever get that close to anyone again. First, there was his Ma and Pa, and now, Maria, his sweet, dear wife. His son would just have to find someone else to look up to. He would never see him again.

The girl came around the corner with a dirty gourd filled with water that looked like it had come from a mud hole. Ryan declined as she held it to his mouth. He turned his face away.

Another man walked around the barn and stood with both hands on his hips glaring down at Ryan. "You come back after my woman! I let you get away last time. I think I'll just shoot you this en." It was the man who had slammed a rifle against Ryan's temple on his last trip through this hog wallow.

"Do whatever you feel like doing. I don't care. Just get it over with."

The man looked curiously at the man seated on the ground with his hands tied behind him. "You don't want my woman? Ain't she good enough fer you? What's a matter with her? She's the purtiest woman in a hunnert miles."

"Probably is. I'm just not interested in women right now. Why don't you just shoot me and get it done. Then we'll all be happy." Ryan could care less. He wanted this world to go away.

The man standing with a rifle, looked down at it and then back to Ryan. He had never had anybody ask him to shoot them before. "Somebody lookin fer you? You done kilt somebody?"

"I guess I did. I killed my wife. That's what I did. I killed my wife! I'm a wife killer! So why don't you just go ahead and shoot me!"

The man looked at him, then at the rifle again, and then at his own wife. He shook his head and walked away around the building.

An hour later, just as the sun was disappearing over the horizon, the woman brought a blue plate filled with some kind of stew and sat it on the ground next to Ryan. "They told me to set you lose. You ain't gonna hurt me is you?"

Ryan looked at her with tear-filled eyes. "I won't hurt you." He rolled on his side away from the woman and began to sob once again. "Maria. Maria."

Chapter Six

Now it came about when he had finished speaking to Saul, that the soul of Jonathan was knit to the soul of David, and Jonathan loved him as himself. 1Samuel 18:1

Jose was just about to dismount and have another one of the cold biscuits when he smelled something in the air. It smelled like smoke. It was near dark again and was beginning to be hard to see. He pondered whether he should go now and find the smoke or wait till morning. He decided to wait.

He cautiously and as quietly as he could, stepped down from the saddle and tethered his horse to a small mesquite bush. He sat on the ground and leaned against the same bush, wanting to feel the closeness of the warm animal. For the third night in a row, Jose would not get much sleep.

Dawn came quicker than he expected and he could still sniff the light aroma of smoke. This time it smelled stale like from an old fire that had been left smoldering overnight. He mounted and rode slowly in the direction of where he thought the smell came from. His eyes darted left and right not wanting to be surprised by an unnoticed assailant.

Ahead of him he could see a cluster of trees and then a cloud of smoke rose into the sky from somewhere in the cluster. Someone was building a fresh fire, and it was not a small one as someone who wanted to remain unseen. Jose shivered in the cold and rode along even more wary. He saw a sod hut through the trees and an old man seated on a makeshift chair hewn from a tree trunk. Jose watched as he guzzled from an earthenware jug between loud, hacking, coughing spells and throwing something at the three dogs who, lay silently in the dirt ignoring him.

Jose looked around the yard and saw no one else about, but he figured someone else had started the fire inside the sod house. He sat astride his horse out of sight in the trees and watched. Soon, he saw a shadow cross the back corner of the house as if someone had left by a rear door. He could not see the door so he moved around through the trees to get a better vantage point.

As he watched a girl slipped out the back door and looking over her shoulder, walked slowly around a building resembling a small horse barn. Still not able to see where she had gone, he changed positions again. This time, halfway to his new position, he heard the distinct sound of a rifle hammer being cocked. At that same moment, he saw a familiar form lying spread out in the dust near the corral.

"You lookin for somethin Mex?" A scroungy looking gringo was standing to his right, pointing the barrel of an old muzzleloader at him.

"Me no comprende. Aqua! Aqua!" Jose pretended not to speak English. "No sabby de englase."

"What you want Mex?" The gringo ignored his request for water.

Jose lifted his canteen, which was near empty after two days of washing down dry biscuits. "Aqua, senor. Aqua."

"You get your Awah outin that horse trough and be on yore way." He pointed to the trough where Ryan lay sprawled out. "I ketch you round here again, I put a ball in yore head. Now git!"

Jose filled his canteen watching Ryan out of the corner of his eye. He did not want to wake his friend at this point or they both may be shot. He filled the canteen as quickly and quietly as he could and walked away, leading his horse. He waited until he was well away from his friend and held the water vessel up toward the gringo. "Mucho gracious." He was grinning from ear to ear, and bowing from the waist.

Jose mounted his horse and rode slowly away from the dilapidated compound and back into the trees. He was well away from the dwelling before he felt courageous enough to stop. Slowly turning his animal to the north, Jose began to circle around and come in from a different direction, this time tying his horse to a tree and moving ahead on foot. He made his way very cautiously, not wanting to alarm the man or woman. The older one was already flaked out in the yard amongst the sleeping dogs.

Ryan's friend was there to rescue him and bring him back to his family. Jose remembered that Ryan had not been bound. *Was he free to leave? Would they move him inside?* He would just have to wait, and watch and find the right opportunity to get him free.

Jose sat most of the day, watching the very little activity going on. The old man never moved from his spot among the hounds. The gringo who had the musket was inside the sod building with the woman. Ryan had stirred once but had not moved from his place near the trough. As he surveyed the area, he found that he might be able to circle around, keeping the barn between himself and the others. Around noon, he ate the last dry biscuit and washed it down with water from the trough he had filled in his canteen with.

He finally devised a plan. He walked his horse toward the barn and water trough and made it to the corner of the barn that was nearest the water. Ryan was only fifteen feet away from him, lying prone and sound asleep. Jose cautiously approached and began to lift Ryan to a standing position. Ryan started muttering and then opened his eyes. When he saw Jose, he tried to pull away and run to the house. Jose was not a large man or a strong man, but he knew he must save his friend. He spoke softly to Ryan so that he would look in his direction, and then hit him on the jaw just as hard as he could. Ryan slumped into his arms and Jose managed to hoist and throw his friend across the saddle and mount behind him.

He heard the gringo yell and felt the hum of a musket ball as it sped past his ear. Jose knew that the man with the rifle could not reload quickly and rode at full gallop away from him. A yell behind him was loud and clear. "Hey you Mex! What did you steal?" Holding Ryan in place, he rode to the west and toward Santa Fe.

"Only my friend." He smiled and looked back.

——————— ….. ———————

In the shadow of a boulder with three small pinion trees Jose helped Ryan from across the saddle and lowered him to the ground. Ryan sat silently and watched his compadre build a fire and set a coffee pot over the flames. Neither of them spoke for a long while and the first one to do so was Jose.

"You must go and see your son, my friend. He will need his Papa. Please my friend I know to grow up with no Mama and Papa." Jose spoke from his own life not knowing his Mama and Papa, but watching them brutally murdered.

"I guess you are right Amigo. I must go see my son." Ryan had tears in his eyes as he spoke. "We will go to Santa Fe at first light manana. You look tired, my friend. Get some sleep."

Jose was very pleased that he had found his friend and that they were going home to Santa Fe to see the baby boy that was Ryan's first born. He had not slept for three nights. Tonight he would get a good rest. "Goodnight Amigo".

Jose woke with the sun well high in the eastern sky. He had slept in the shadow of the boulder and did not see it come up. The lack of sleep had caused him to sleep hard and long past daylight. Ryan would have the coffee pot already going. He rubbed the sleep from his eyes and looked to where he had built a fire the day before. There were cold ashes.

There was no fire, no coffee, and no Ryan. He had left Jose stranded alone in a cool desert morning. The horse was gone. All the food, water and even the pot to make coffee. Jose was alone in the middle of nowhere not knowing which way to go. He finally gathered his thoughts and walked the camp until he found the tracks his horse had left. Ryan was not headed back to Santa Fe, but to the east and on to Texas.

Jose decided at that moment. If he were going to die in the desert, it would be following his friend and not giving up until he had brought him home to his Bambino.

———————— ..... ————————

Three days later a gasping thirsty and weather-beaten young Mexican staggered into a small, quiet settlement. There was no town, only a gathering of adobe structures loosely encircling a freshwater spring that spilled over a large portal that resembled a Spanish Hacienda's front veranda. It was like a miracle to Jose. It would be the first water his parched dry lips had savored in three days. Before he drank from the cool cascading stream of liquid, he fell to his knees and thanked the Lord for this blessing. He lowered his head and let the cold refreshing spring tumble over his head and all over his hot dry body. Even in the late October desert, his body was drying out from lack of water. When he had consumed his fill of the life renewing fluid, he rolled onto his back and looked to the heavens. *Ryan. He must continue on to find his friend.*

He turned and saw three young Mexican ninos silhouetted in the blazing sun. They stared down at the stranger who lay soaking in the cool of a pinion tree.

"You know if a gringo passed this way on a Cayuse?"

"Si. Gringo fill Aqua and go." One of the boys pointed to the southwest.

"That is right senor. The Gringo take the Aqua and go. Not even say adios." A man wearing a sombrero similar to the one that Jose wore spoke to him from the shadows of the nearest cabana. "You look like you could eat some frijoles and tortillas. Si?"

Si was the right word. Jose had not eaten for three days except for some cactus pears he tried to peel with a rock. Ryan had even taken his knife. "Si. I will eat your frijoles and tortillas and praise the Lord."

Jose thanked his host and packed with what food they could provide, and a skin filled with the cool spring water, he started off in the tracks of his own horse, following after his friend. In a short time, he came upon a marker that pronounced that he had entered the great state of Texas.

He had only been in Texas one time, working a chuck wagon for Mister Charles Goodnight, following a herd of longhorns to the Palo Dura Canyon. He had to leave the drive, because men were on his trail trying to kill him. This time he was trying to find a friend and bring him home.

Chapter Seven

Let love of the brethren continue. Do not neglect to show hospitality to strangers, for by this some have entertained angels without knowing it. Hebrews 13:1,2

Four men rode out of Bandera with a packhorse following along behind them. They were riding toward Waco because they were not sure where the Lord was leading them. It took them four days of riding and praying to decide that Waco was not where the Lord was sending them. Following the trail that Jesse Chisholm had carved, they came upon Salado creek and bedded down outside the stage depot that had been created by the trail of the cattle.

When they had crossed over the creek and forty miles short of Waco, the Lord turned them to the northwest and brought them along a river none of them never had heard of. Not even Ben, who had driven cattle near Waco when he rode with Jesse Chisholm on their first trail drive. The river had a peculiar name to them all. It was called the Bosque. In Spanish, the word meant woods or wooded. Both banks of the clear stream were covered with scrub oaks and lots of cedar trees.

At the end of the first day, they rode into a settlement called Valley Mills. The serene little town was located on the north bank of the river, so they forded at a shallow spot just downstream of a flourmill that was powered by the flowing waters of the river. There was quite a bit of activity as they clambered up the riverbank and turned west into the village. In the middle of the town's main street, several women were gathered around tables that were set up They seemed to be preparing some sort of meal and the whole town showed up to eat.

No one noticed the four riders among all the laughter and fun that was going on.

Jonah asked one of the men who walked by them eating some sort of sweet bread. "Excuse me mister. What's going on?"

"You must be new in town." He looked at the other three. "You all must be new. Once a year we shut down the mill and the women make Norwegian pancakes and cook good Norwegian sausage all day long. Help yourself. Them women love to feed us menfolk."

All four looked at each other and then at the tables stacked high with food. Trail food was nothing compared to a woman's home cooking. They fell into a line behind several other hungry men. Two women looked at them expectantly, and one asked. "Where's your plate?"

The four strangers had forgotten to remove plates or cups from their saddlebags, and now were embarrassed.

"That's alright Sarah. We got extras." One of the other women reached across the table and handed them plates stacked high with round, ball shaped pancakes and several links of white colored sausage links.

Another woman poured cups of hot steaming coffee. "Fresh strawberry preserves on that table." She pointed them in the direction of a table covered with jars of various fruit preserves and syrups.

The four hungry men made their way across and spooned on an assortment of flavors atop the round cakes, then found a place to sit on a boardwalk.

"Is this the place that the Lord sent us?" Johnny asked, while he was spooning another mouthful of preserves.

"Don't know. We'll have to wait and see." Jonah replied.

After they had eaten their fill, the stuffed young men walked around the small town. It was a peaceful little community nestled on the bank of the Bosque River. Everyone seemed to be so friendly. Almost everyone they passed asked the same question. "Get enough to eat?"

They circled the town and went back to where their horses were tied to a hitching rail. Untying the animals they strolled down the street to the livery and fed, and watered them.

All of them including the horses had a good day at the feed trough. They made their way down the street and out of town on the west side, finding a quiet peaceful spot under an extra-large oak tree. They setup camp for the day. The sun was twinkling through the tree leaves as they bedded down for the night.

———————— ..... ————————

All four of them had wondered if that was where the Lord had intended for them to speak to the people about building a church. When the new day came, it was obvious that this town did not need a new church. It was Sunday and everyone in town was walking to the small chapel they had seen in the center of the small settlement

It would be a day of rest for the travelers along the sedate riverbank. They all put on their Sunday best and joined the townsfolk in a morning of worship. Several invitations to eat at homes had been offered and they found it difficult to say no, but they did not want to hurt anyone's feeling. They settled back on the riverbank and spent the afternoon discussing which way to go. While they drank coffee and read from the Bible, two women approached with Cherry pies they could not decline.

One of the women spoke up. "If you want a place to talk to people about God, you may try Clifton up the river. It used to be a good town, but some bad men have moved in there. They closed the church and don't use it anymore."

The answer, they were seeking had just been given to them.

On a bright cool Monday morning, the four speakers of the word rode out with a new confidence in what they were doing. Only a one-day ride up the Bosque River was the answer to their prayers.

———————— ..... ————————

It was almost noon and they were enjoying a relaxed ride along the cool waters of the Bosque. They had to be in no hurry, so they stopped to drink a cup of coffee and eat the cherry pie the women from Valley Mills had given them. While they ate, they discussed the possibilities that awaited them in Clifton.

The sound of a horse coming along the riverbank, suddenly alerted them to danger. Johnny reached for his weapon and stood next to one of the oak trees back from the bank. The sound ceased as if the horse had stopped.

All of them listened intently for the animal to start moving again. When it did not Jonah motioned to Ben and Abe to circle around and come in upstream of where they had heard the noise. He put his finger to his lips and motioned Johnny to stay put. He began to ease along the bank, keeping trees between him and whatever might be there.

Abe and Ben slipped through the trees and found their way to the bank two hundred yards upstream of their fire sight. They cautiously made their way along until a horse, standing alone near the river, came into view.

They looked in all directions and then saw Jonah easing along from the south side of the animal. He saw them and they all shrugged their shoulders. Each continued toward the horse until Jonah, from his vantage point saw a man lying on the ground at the horse's feet. Jonah holstered his weapon and moved closer to the man. He was lying face down and was unconscious. Abe and Ben came to where Jonah was bending over the man, and Abe called to Johnny. Johnny slowly made his way to where the others were.

Jonah rolled the unconscious man over onto his back. His face was severely beaten and swollen. There were cut marks all over his head. "He's been pistol whipped." Jonah looked up at the other men.

The man began to move around and make groaning sounds.

"Let's get him to the fire." Ben reached out to help Jonah lift him and they carried him the short distance to the fire they had made for coffee.

By the time they got him there, he was waking and looking around; He drew back from the strangers with fear in his eyes. "No! Don't hit me again. I didn't see anything. Please."

"We won't hurt you. Take it easy. Who did this to you?"

"Don't you work for the mayor? I don't know you."

"No, we don't work for the mayor. We haven't been to town yet." Jonah spoke to the frightened man. "What happened to you? It is obvious someone beat you, but who and why? We are sent to Clifton to help rebuild the church. Is that what this is about?"

"It was Rance Martin. He came into town, stuffed the ballot, and got himself elected mayor. The preacher spoke out and this is what happened. He beat the preacher too. I don't even know if he is still alive. All I did was see him set the fire. He saw me too. That's why he gun whipped me. I managed to find my way to a horse and get out of town."

The four warriors looked at each other, Johnny spoke. "I think we better get into town. Sounds like they need help."

"Are you okay mister? We'll leave you here if you are. If you feel like riding, you can go back with us."

"I think I'll stay here for a while. Any coffee in that pot?"

Abe poured him a cup and then the four of them mounted and headed west into the town of Clifton.

Chapter Eight

We heard him say, I will destroy this temple made with hands, and within three days I will build another without hands
Mark 14:58

Loud noise emanated from a saloon as the four rode into the town of Clifton. Like Valley Mills, it was on the north bank of the Bosque River, and there was a flourmill similar to the other. That is where the similarities for the two towns ended. Both towns were probably friendly but in a different sort of way. All of them had been in towns where they left you alone, as long as you went along with the wild and wooly ways of the town's bad boys.

Jonah, Ben, Abe, and Johnny rode slowly and silently through the main street of Clifton and like in Valley Mills found a quiet, peaceful place on the river to set up camp. Across the river, there was a high limestone cliff, rising above the landscape. They made sure they camped so the trees would offer some protection from sight and gunfire from up on the cliffs.

At one time, they would have had to be on the watch for Indians, but now most of them had been subdued by army forces and delegated to reservations. Most of them were in Oklahoma.

Caddo, Tawakoni, Tonkawa, Tow ash, and a few Waco still were around, but they lived peacefully with the whites. Some of them had learned to farm and planted a wheat crop that was milled by one of the local mills.

Most of the Indians lived in cone shaped, thatch covered, structures similar to the teepees they used when they were still in traveling bands. They spent their time, when not working the fields, sitting on thatch-covered sofas inside their dwellings. The sofa's, were positioned around the wall of the dwelling, and served as a seat and a place to sleep.

It was late afternoon, so Jonah and the others set up camp and had a meal and coffee. They decided it would be best to wait til morning to walk the town while the entire bad element was still asleep.

They were right. When they strolled down the main street, in the following early light, there was no one about. Around one of the corners down a side street, they found a recently burned building.

In the rubble were the remains of a cross that had once sat upon a steeple.

"What are you looking for? Haven't you done enough?" A quivering voice came out of the shadows of a nearby house. It was the voice of a woman.

"Yes ma'am. I'm looking for a place to pray to my Lord." Abe spoke.

"Ma'am do you know where the preacher lives?" It was Ben this time.

"Why do you ask?" She sounded frightened.

"Because we came to this town to make sure a new church gets started. He should be the one to talk to." This time Jonah spoke out with a loud voice.

"Sir? Are you some of the men who work for the mayor, Mister Martin?" Again her voice trembled.

"I don't know your Mayor, ma'am, but if he did this, we all will know him soon." Johnny spoke for the first time expressing the feelings of them all.

"My husband is the Pastor. This is where we live. He is hurt and cannot come out to talk to you." The woman began to weep.

"May we come in and speak to your husband. We mean you no harm." Jonah spoke in a softer speech.

The woman looked up and down the street. "Please, don't let anyone see you. Quickly now, come in."

The four of them also looked at the street, and then walked quickly to where the preacher's wife held a door wide for them.

When they had entered the small two-room house, the woman directed them to the back room where a man was lying on his back in a sagging bed.

"Martha. Who is that Martha?" Both the man's eyes were blackened shut, and his face was cut and had been bleeding. He tried to get up.

"Lie down preacher. We are here to help. We will not harm you or your wife. Believe me. The Lord sends us. Everything will be alright." Jonah again spoke in a gentler voice.

"Who are you? How did you know?"

"I am Jonah Smith. These are my compadres, Ben Stark, Abe Tobias, and young Johnny Warren. How did we know? An angel at Valley Mills told us. That is all you need to know for now. We are camped at the north edge of the town. If you need us, send someone. If we're not there look for us in town. We won't be hard to find. Right now we have work to do." Jonah saw the look of relief come over the man's face and then walked to the other room.

"Oh praise the Lord." The preacher's wife was still shedding a flood of tears. "My name is Martha Lane. My husband is James Lane. We have not been here long. We are new to the ministry."

"So are we Ma'am. If you need us, send someone." Jonah was trying to reassure her.

"Mister Smith, did you see Mister Johnson. He saw the mayor set the fire and got beaten with a handgun. He tried to go for help." Martha Lane was concerned for one of their congregation.

"Mister Johnson is alright ma'am. We found him. In the meantime, try to remember everyone else in the preacher's congregation. We'll want to talk to them."

"There are only eight of us." She spoke as if she was embarrassed.

"The Lord only had twelve. With us, that's how many you have."

———— ..... ————

    The best two places in any small western town to get information is the saloon or the post office. Since none of them took to drinking, the first place was the post office. That is where they would start. In a small town like Clifton, the post office would be in the general store. The four of them walked side by side down the boardwalk until they came to a door with almost as many people going in and out as the saloon. That would be the place.

    There was a potbellied stove to one side of the store with a wire-covered window nearby. Over the window were the words U. S. Post office. Jonah looked around and found a small man wearing a sun visor over his eyes. He looked like the official postmaster. He approached the man and spoke loudly so everyone could hear... ""When is the next election in this town for mayor?"

"Well, not for a while. We just elected one." The man responded.

"I think you need to elect a new one. I hear this one burns churches down." Most of the people either looked away or left the store. Jonah was sure one of them was on his way to the mayor's office right now.

"Do any of you go to the church that was burned?" Abe asked the question.

"How about it. Any of you go to Reverend Lane's church?" This time it was Ben.

"Well, speak up. Any of you good people go to church? "Johnny Warren spoke up too. No one answered.

Jonah turned back to the postmaster. "Do you post notices on that board outside your store?"

"Well, yes, if they pertain to business." He tried to look official, and then cleared his throat.

"I have one for you to post. Write this down. Church meeting tonight at seven p.m. It will be where the mayor burned the church down."

The postmaster hesitated.

"You get it all?"

"I can't post that!"

"Why not? It is town business. If that is not good enough, sign it. Jonah Caleb Smith, U. S. Territorial Marshall. These three men are my deputy Marshalls. I hear tell that new mayor you good people elected, Mister Rance Martin, is wanted over in San Antonio."

A low buzz spread throughout those remaining in the store and all of them began to leave. Some were trying to be nonchalant until they were outside and then left quickly to go spread the news.

"Anyone sees the mayor, invite him to the meeting. We'll have a prayer time, just for him." Jonah stepped out the front door followed by his friends.

When they walked out into the street, five men stepped off the boardwalk in front of the saloon. They spread out across the street and watched the four men who had left the store. Each one of them lifted their revolvers and slid it in and out of his holsters to make sure they were ready to pull.

Jonah, Ben Abe, and Johnny looked down the street and saw the men coming, and spread themselves across the street facing their adversaries. Jonah spoke. "You men work for the mayor, I guess. What are you going to do when he loses his job and leaves town? " "If you have been in San Antonio you should know me. My name is Jonah Smith."

One of the men near the boardwalk on the other side of the street recognized the name. He stopped and looked at one of the others. "I ain't getting paid to shoot no Marshall!"

He walked to the hitching rail and mounted his horse. One of the other men mumbled something to the man who had spoken to Jonah, and then he turned and walked off down the street.

"Now, who is outnumbered?" Ben asked the man.

"Yeh, let's get this over with. You boy's ready to do this? Johnny gambled they would not fight.

"You Jonah Smith?" The man they thought to be the leader asked.

"You want to find out? Make a move." Abe stared at the man, his hand hanging at his side near his revolver.

"Marshall, we didn't have anything to do with that church. We just came to town lookin for a job. We needed work. We don't want no trouble."

"Then I think you ought to go somewhere else." Jonah spoke very sternly.

The three men looked at each other, turned, went quickly to their mounts, saddled, and rode out of town.

The four new arrivals in town spent the rest of the day walking around town, visiting with everyone that would speak to them. That number began to grow as the day went on.

By evening people were beginning to mill around the sight of the church burning. The Parson was brought onto the tiny front porch of their house and seated on a bench. At seven o'clock one of the towns people clanged on a bell that had been salvaged from the church.

Jonah and the three men with him stepped forward to begin the meeting. "Did the mayor make it? Anyone invite the mayor, Mister Martin?" Jonah looked over the crowd.

Someone in the rear spoke up. "Yeh, I told him to come. I told him who you were. He said he had to go to Waco. Said he might not make it back out this way for a while. A round of applause went up and Jonah held his hands high...

"I think it's time to sing. Miss Martha, can you lead us in a song. "Ben touched the preacher's wife on the shoulder.

"Hey preacher. We can have church in that old rock school house." Someone called out. Martha stepped up and spoke quietly. "I'll try to sing if you all help. I heard a missionary say one time. Expect great things from God. Attempt great things for God. That is what these four men are doing. I think we should thank them and pray for them."

Chapter Nine

*There is an appointed time for everything. And there is a time for every event under heaven- A time to give birth and a time to die: A time to plant and a time to uproot what is planted.
Ecclesiastes 3:1,2*

Spotted Fawn walked back and forth across the front of their small cabin at the headwaters of the Rio Grande. She had already walked a path in the layer of snow that had covered the ground the night before. She kept peering into the higher elevations looking for any sign of a rider towing a packhorse.

Fawn was waiting for Samson, her husband of twelve years to return from a trip up into the San Juan Mountains to check his traps. Their son, Samson Castile Raines was around behind the cabin chopping firewood for his mother.

Samson had been gone for almost two months and Fawn was worried something had happened to him. He usually didn't take this long to check the few traps that he still ran. The beaver were getting to be sparse in the Colorado Mountains. Sam was one of the few men who still trapped the elusive animal.

Earlier Fawn had seen movement alongside the downriver trail that followed along the bank of the Rio Grande. It moved in and out of the tree line and only spottily was in her view. Sam would not normally come from that direction but from upstream out of the mountain path.

Sam Raines and Spotted Fawn had come together along the Texas end of the Rio Grande River while Sam was making his way to the mountains to get away from the ravages of the civil war. Fawn had been in and out of Sam's trail, helping him, when he was shot by Apaches and attacked by others outlaws along the way. Sam never knew she was there until she nursed him through a bad snakebite and broken leg right after he crossed from Texas into New Mexico. A sidewinder struck him and he had gone into a delirious state.

Comancheros killed her Grandfather; Walks like a Coyote shortly after that.

Sam found himself falling in love with the young Tonkawa maiden. Sam was the best friend of her uncle Castile, who was a Tonkawa chieftain who had spent the last winter of his life trapping with Samson in the Big Bend Mountains of south Texas.

Spotted Fawn and Sam had come to this place and settled with their friends, Charley Reynolds, and his Ute wife Blue Sparrow. Over the years, the two couples had become very close. Charley had been the one who talked Sam into staying and helping with the ranch.

Charley and Blue Sparrow had gone to visit with what remained of Blue Sparrow's family on a reservation on the East slope of the San Juan Mountains. They would not be home before Sam returned from his traps.

Shading her eyes with one hand, Spotted Fawn squinted down the river trying to make out the forms moving along the trail. Sam would be alone trailing a pack animal behind to carry the beaver pelts. There were two horses coming but both seemed to be mounted with riders. She watched warily glancing toward the mountain trail hoping to see Sam coming home.

Cas, the eleven-year-old son of Spotted Fawn and Sam, came around the corner of the cabin. He had also seen the riders coming up the river

"Who is it Ma?" He looked at Spotted Fawn with a curiosity in his eyes.

"I'm not sure Cas. Looks like two men. Did you put the wood inside?"

"Not yet Ma. I wanted to see who it was."

"You go put the wood by the fireplace, then bring me the rifle. Go on now!" She pushed him toward the cabin. She was very proud of the boy that had come from her and Sam, and so was Sam. Next year, Cas would be old enough to go with his father up into the mountains to run the traps. Sam had taken the boy on short trips and taught him the ways of the Beaver. He was training his son to know the mountains just as his dear friend Castile had taught him.

The riders crossed the river at a shallow spot one hundred yards downstream and rode straight toward the cabin. They were close enough now for Spotted Fawn to know that she did not know them.

Cas walked slowly through the front door and approached his mother with the Henry lever action. One of the riders fired a shot and hit Cas in his lower right arm near the hand that was holding the gun. He dropped the weapon, grabbed his arm, and looked at his mother with a pain on his face.

Spotted Fawn reached for the weapon and yelled to her young son. "Run Cas! Run! Don't stop!" Another shot rang out and a bullet penetrated the upper right shoulder of the brave woman. "Go Cas! Go! Find your father!" The shot had twisted her around and she called to her son over her wounded shoulder.

The wide-eyed young boy ran around the corner of the cabin as another bullet chipped a log near his right ear. He started across the field behind the house and felt searing pain in his left shoulder as a projectile pierced his side between his arm and the fleshy part of his rib cage. He pitched forward and fell face first into the crust of white snow. He tried to raise his head and look back to his mother as he lost consciousness.

Cas was better off to not be able to see what the two strangers had in store for his mother. Spotted

Fawn attempted to run away, but her wound would not allow her to move fast enough to get away. One of the two men ran her down and with his horse knocked her from her feet. The other man dismounted and pulled her to her feet, dragging her toward the front door of the cabin. He had a wide grin on his face and a long, jagged scar over his right eye.

When she stumbled into the front room, she found a knife and slashed at the man who had pushed her inside. She cut across his chest but only caught the front of his shirt. He hit her across the temple with a hard, full fist and knocked her to the floor. She tried to struggle to her feet and he slapped her down again. His cohort limped in behind him and the two of them proceeded to strip her of the deerskin dress that covered her.

After two hours, Cas began to partially gain consciousness. At first, he was unaware of where he was and what had occurred.

When he did come around, he struggled to his knees and supporting himself on one hand, looked toward the cabin, trying to clear his eyes and find his mother. Smoke filled his nostrils and what he saw was his home in full blaze with flames reaching high into the early spring sky. He tried to crawl to help his mother and fell into unconsciousness again.

---·····---

Sam was looking forward to getting back to the cabin and seeing his wife and son. He had been gone nearly two months and the Beaver pelts were few. He was slowly making his way along the path to his home and began anxiously looking for smoke from the chimney.

All of a sudden, he saw a wisp of smoke rise near where his cabin should be. Watching the trail in front of him, he glanced occasionally toward the smoke. Something did not look right to him. The smoke from a chimney should rise straight into the heavens. What he saw was a wide cloud smoldering lazily close to the ground. He made his way to flat ground and dropped the reins of the packhorse. Kicking his horse in the ribs, he prodded his mount into a full gallop. When he was closer, Sam realized that his home had been burned to the ground. *Where is Fawn? Where is Cas?* It seemed to take forever to cross the edge of the river, splashing through the crust of ice on the bank. He jumped from the animals back before it could stop and ran to where the front door should be. The crumbled logs still smoldered and put out an extreme heat that was too intense for him to get to the inside.

"Fawn! Fawn!" He called out to his wife. "Fawn!" Sam began to run around the cabin looking for her. "Cas! Cas!" He yelled his son's name as he ran.

He had circled the cabin three times trying to find his family, when he saw a movement off to the back edge of the flat fifty yards behind the burned out structure. Sam stood still and stared at the movement trying to decipher what he was seeing through tear-filled eyes.

Another movement sent him into a run to what looked like a body struggling on the ground. When he drew close, he realized it was his son Cas. Sam dropped to the side of the injured boy.

"Cas. Cas? Where's your mother? Are you alright?" Sam could see that his son had been shot twice and he needed to help him. "Stay here boy; I'll get something to fix your wounds."

Sam looked around for the pony he had ridden in. The horse was standing away from the smoldering fire trying to nuzzle through the snow cover to get to the roots below. Sam ran to him and grabbed his possibles bag from behind the saddle.

He raised Cas's shirt to look at the worst injury. The shot had gone through the flesh but had creased a rib and cracked the bone. Sam splashed water from his canteen and washed the dried blood away. Cas recoiled at the pain.

"It'll be okay son. I'll wrap it and then look at the other one." He had seen the wound on the boy's arm. "Cas. Try to think. Where did you last see your mother?"

"They shot her Pa!"

"Where? Where was she? Think son."

"In front. She told me to run! I'm sorry Pa! She told me to run and I ran! I should have stayed with her!" Tears began streaming down the youngsters cheeks.

"It's not your fault son. Just try to think. Did you know who it was?"

"No Pa. I never saw them before. Ma didn't either. She told me to go get the Henry. When I got it, one of them shot me in the arm. That's when Ma told me to run." Tears welled in his eyes again. "Then they shot her and I ran, but they shot me in the back."

Sam stood and helped Cas to his feet. He looked to the ranch house that Charley and Blue Sparrow called home. He knew they would not be there, or this would not have happened.

Sam helped Cas to his horse and when he was saddled, walked him to the house that was still standing. He helped his son down and carried him into the home of Charley and Blue Sparrow. Sam laid Cas onto a bed in the room where he and Spotted Fawn had spent their first night on the ranch.

The man who wanted to be left alone, sat with his son until he was sleeping. He walked to the front window and looked out at the smoldering ash that had been his home, with his wife and son. *Who would want to destroy that?*

Sam checked to see that Cas was still sleeping and walked out and mounted the horse and rode slowly back to where his wife and son had been shot. He sat for a moment, surveyed the pile of destruction, and looked around the ranch as far as he could see, trying to see Spotted Fawn. She was nowhere to be seen. He looked back to the ash and stepped down. Slowly and meticulously, he circled the fallen cabin looking for any sign of his wife.

Finally, over in a back corner, Sam saw a piece of doeskin that covered a burned body. The form was unrecognizable, but Sam knew. He lowered his head. "Why God? What have I done? I pray to you! I read your Word! Why? " Sam fell to his knees and released the torment and tears that he had been holding within himself. The broken man kneeled on the ground with his head in his hands and cried for an hour. He never once blamed God or cursed him for what had happened.

Sam struggled to his feet and wiped his eyes on the back of a sleeve. He looked to the house where his son laid suffering from gunshot wounds. He must carry out his responsibility. He must take care of his son. Sam made himself walk into the ashes and retrieve what was left of Spotted Fawn. He dug a grave under the pinion tree where Cas was born and laid his true love to rest.

He led the mount back to the house to check on Cas. When he walked into the room the boy was still sleeping. Sam lay beside his son and closed his eyes, but he did not sleep.

When the morning light shown through the window, Cas stirred and it alerted Sam.

"Pa? Pa? "

"I'm here Son. You ready to eat something?" Sam knew that the boy needed to keep up his strength.

"Pa. Where's Ma? Did you find Ma?" Cas looked into his father's eyes with expectation.

"Yes. I found your Ma, Cas. Cas she's gone. That's all you need to know." Sam looked away as tears started to well up in his eyes again.

"What are we going to do Pa?"

"Do you know what those two men look like, Cas" Sam turned to face his son again.

Yessir. I seen both of them! We going to go get them Pa! I know them! One had a bad limp. The one that chased Ma had a scar on his head right here!" He drug his hand across his forehead above his right eye. "When we going to leave Pa?"

"When you get good to travel and Charley and Blue Sparrow get home. We can't leave them not knowing what happened.

Chapter Ten

> Your sons shall be shepherds for forty years in the wilderness, and they will suffer for your unfaithfulness, until your corpses lie in the wilderness. Numbers 14:43

Llano Estacado was a wide grassy plain that covered most of west Texas and parts of New Mexico. It went as far north as the Canadian River covering a vast expanse of thirty seven thousand miles. It was bordered on the east by the Cap rock Escarpment, outlined by a three hundred foot cliff. On the west was Mescalero Escarpment extending to the Pecos River Valley. To the south, the plain merged into the landscape. There was very little water to be found anywhere on the flat arid plain.

Ryan Hale rode into a canyon that was occupied by only one building. A dingy yellow-sided structure was virtually falling down. Only two long poles on one side held it into place. A sign was hanging precariously under an overhang that served as a front porch. The words were hard to make out, but he finally realized it read Lubbock Post Office

Ryan had just crossed the largest share of Llano Estacado. He was fast running out of water and looked around for a place to find a drink for him and his horse. There were few places to find the cool liquid on the grassy plain.

He did find one place that someone had dug deep enough to leave a sign of parched earth to indicate there was water if you dug deep abundantly. Down on his knees, the dry and thirsty man dug with his hands until he created a layer of mud. He tried to squeeze a handful to get a drop onto his tongue, to no benefit. A little deeper and he found a small trickle of water and watched it pool just enough to slurp it with his tongue. His mouth was still swollen and so were his eyes, but he had to allow the deep breathing animal that had brought him there to try to lap water from the seepage.

By the time he reached Lubbock Post Office, Ryan had galloped for three days since he left Jose Gonzales stranded in the dry lands of New Mexico, and once more, had ridden a horse to near collapse.

Dismounting with difficulty, he strode into the dilapidated yellow building and found no one around. Pinned to a rusty cage was a note. This is Thursday, be back Monday if any mail shows up.

There was no sign of water and not a soul around to show him where to find it. Ryan looked around, then painfully stuck his left foot into a stirrup and slowly lifted his leg over the cantle and settled into the saddle.

Ryan did not care what happened to him now. If that was what the Lord wanted, he would ride back into the grasslands and let God send him to hades!

He turned his horse to the north and headed toward whatever fate awaited him. The terrain did not change and the water was still not to be had. He didn't care.

Riding on, he began to choke on the dry powdery swelling in his mouth. The mount began to stagger along, barely able to put one foot in front of the other.

Ryan leaned forward over the Concho side of his saddle. He was beginning to see hallucinations. A huge lake loomed in front of him and he spurred the horse and tried to yell at him, but no sound came out of his lips. The animal did not respond, so Ryan slid to the side, dropped from the horses back, and fell hard into the tall grass. Once more, the Lord had abandoned him. He rolled onto his back and stared through blurred vision into the heavens. The sun was bright in the sky, even for an early November day.

"Get it done God! Don't you think I've suffered enough?" He tried once again to raise his voice and once again, nothing came forth from his mouth. He rolled his head away from the sky and stared into the tall brown grass. *This is it! This is where the pain ends.*

Ryan closed his severely swollen eyes and waited for the end.

The sound of a horse whicker brought him back to life. Ryan did not know how long he had been there. He tried to open his eyes, but they were tightly swollen shut. Someone slipped a hand behind his neck and, lifting him, poured a trickle of water over his lips. He tried to suck in the liquid and the flow stopped. A wet cloth began wiping at his wind burned and blistered face. The cooling water relaxed him and he lay back onto the dry grass. He heard someone stand and walk away. The footsteps were soft and quiet and Ryan knew they wore moccasins.

An arm wrapped around his waist and two people lifted him, carried him to a horse, and laid him across the saddle. Rawhide wrapped around his wrist and someone reached under and slung the thong around his boots.

The next thing he remembered was being carefully lowered from the mount and being carried for a short distance to a place that was cool and damp. His eyes were still swollen, but he was beginning to see slivers of light through the slits. He went to sleep and for the first time in weeks fell into a deep slumber. They had brought his mount into the damp opening in the side of a cliff and removed its saddle.

His eyes were opening some wider when he woke and he could see movement around a low flickering flame. One of the two men saw he was awake and brought him a crock bowl with beans and flat bread.

"You eat!" The bowl was thrust at him.

Ryan took the bowl of food and squinted, holding it close to his face to try to see what it was. He had forgotten how hungry he was and how long it had been since he had eaten.

"What white man do in Ar--mah-Ree-yuh?" One of the two spoke to him.

"Ar- mah- Ree -yuh? What is Ar- mah- Ree-yuh?"

"White man not know yellow flower?"

"This white man not know yellow flower. What is yellow flower?" Ryan could not see good enough to figure out who they were, but they had to be red men by their talk and the fact that they called him white man.

"Where am I?" Ryan did not know yellow flower and where it was.

"You know Palo Duro?" The other one asked this time.'

"Yes, I know Palo Duro" Ryan remembered that the Charles Goodnight herd was headed to Palo Duro Canyon and he had trailed Jose Gonzales to there, only to lose him.

"This lands our land! We not go with Quanah Parker to reservation!" The next one to speak spoke loudly and forcefully.

"We kill all white men who come here!" The second one almost yelled.

"Why did you not kill me?" Ryan did not care at this point if they did kill him.

"We no kill loco mans. You loco. You talk to sky. We give aqua. We give food. We turn loose. You go be more loco." With that, the Comanche Indians left the small cave and Ryan to fend for himself.

Without food or water, Ryan made his way up the canyon and felt the cold winds of winter as he climbed above the high walls and once again rode across the grassy plain. His horse had recovered from the mistreatment his master had put him through and was able to stride through the tall grass.

Storm clouds moved slowly across the sky and the rumble of thunder filled the air. There was the smell of moisture in the gentle wind that cooled Ryan's face. It smelled like a flower mingled with rain. Must be the wind 's of Ah-mah-Ree- yuh. He recalled what the red men had asked him about the yellow flower.

Ryan guided his mount to the east and four days later came to the edge of a small settlement. He had no idea where he was. There was a sign mounted on a tilted post stuck into the dry, parched ground and grown nearly over by the same brown grass across which he had just rode. He dismounted and walked into the street, leading the animal behind him.

The nearly delirious man, half-walking, half stumbling, squinted through blistered eyes down a wide street that seemed to be lined with structures on both side. He staggered along until he heard the sound of a piano blaring from inside one of the building.

Ryan threw the reins over what he saw as a hitching rail, and struggled up two steps to a boardwalk. Raindrops mixed with particles of ice pelted against his back as he walked to the door. He did not turn to see the storm that was coming.

Laughter greeted him as he made his way through the double doors into a smoke filled room.

The odor that emanated from the stranger caused other men to give way and watch as he clumsily stumbled his way to the bar.

"Can I have a drink?' He spoke to the bartender through parched lips, licking them with a tongue that was just as desperate for a drink.

"We got whiskey! You want whiskey?" The man across the bar recoiled as Ryan spoke.

"Water, I need water."

"We got whiskey. You want water, there's a trough out front. Mister, while you're out there get in that trough and take yourself a bath, or stand out there in that rain that's coming You stink."

"I want a drink of whiskey!" Ryan had never before let the foul taste of alcohol pass his lips.

"You got any money?" The barman looked at him quizzically.

Ryan fumbled through his pockets and came up with nothing. "I need a drink. Please?"

One of the men standing down the bar spoke up. "Give him a drink Morris. He looks like he needs it."

The man behind the bar grumbled. "He needs a bath more", as he poured a shot glass full with whiskey.

Ryan picked up the glass and turned it to his burned lips. He poured it all down a blistered throat and felt warmth that he had never felt before. Even with the pain it caused, it made him feel good.

"Pour me another." He dropped the glass back onto the bar.

The bartender looked down the way to the man who had bought the first one. The man dipped his chin and the second in a long line of drinks flowed down the throat of a man who had given up on life and his God.

Chapter Eleven

There is a shelter to give shade from the heat by day, and refuge and protection from the storm and rain. Isaiah 4:6

Jose Gonzales sat on a clump of brown grass that had been piled high by the elements, rubbing his blistered feet. He was uncertain whether he could get his well worn, boots back on. He was also not sure of which way to go. The water skin was nearly dry of the water he had filled it with back at the fresh water spring in New Mexico. Looking in all directions, he managed to force his feet into his boots and stand. There was a new tightness as he took the first few steps. He could feel a chill in the air as storm clouds approached from the southwest. His direction was decided for him. He walked to the northeast away from the storm.

Struggling through the tall dry grass, he continued until he came to the walls of a deep canyon. The wind was getting a fierceness about it and Jose began looking for shelter. He climbed down over the edge of craggy rocks and began a descent into the canyon walls. Halfway down he saw a small cavern under an outcropping and crawled into it out of the coming storm. He found a small stream of rain dripping between two rocks. Jose positioned the water skin, and waited for drops to fill it with fresh cool liquid.

Jose curled up into a ball, closed his eyes, and waited for a restful sleep to come over him. He was cold, but he had managed to find a place to be dry. Jose wondered about his friend Ryan and hoped he was going in the right direction to find and help him.

The storm was furious and lasted all that day and most of the night. When Jose woke, it was still dark and heavy rain and hail was washing streams down into the canyon. Rocks tumbled down and clattered against each other on their way to the floor far below. He felt as if he were under a waterfall as the water cascaded over the overhang above him.

Jose shook off a chill and closed his eyes again and went back to sleep. This time when he woke the rain had stopped and the streams had slowed to trickles and the waterfall was no longer spilling over his head. He picked up his water skin and took a long deep swallow of the cold fresh, clean rainwater.

Looking down into the canyon, he saw a river flowing in a winding torrent along the floor. Longhorn steers were milling along the banks with a shocked, dazed, look in their eyes.

Jose climbed over rocks loosened by the rain and hand over hand made his way out of the precipice. When he stood on the top edge, he smelled a new freshness in the air. It smelled like fresh picked flowers. He remembered the smell from his child hood, when he had seen his mother pick them. That was a long time ago and before he saw his parents die at the hands of the Apache.

The grass was still wet and hard to walk in as he followed the curvature of the canyon rim. He stayed close to the edge and managed to find some rocky terrain to help his excursion. Finally, the gorge disappeared behind him and he was once more on the flat grassy plain. He circled around and continued his walk to the northeast.

Near sundown, ten days later, he saw the lights of a town on the horizon and using them for a guide, stumbled along in the darkness. He made the edge of town and saw a sign hanging on a post that was about to fall over in the wet soil.

Jose, not wanting to be seen found his way along the street until he found a livery. There was no one on the street and the only sound was laughter coming from the many saloons. up and down the street. He crossed the street as he passed by so he wouldn't run into anyone. He made his way down an alley and quietly entered the livery by the back door, standing to listen for a moment to make sure no one was there. Feeling his way along a wall, he felt his way past two horses and came upon a ladder. He climbed into a hay-filled loft, covered himself with the fresh smelling hay, and once again dozed into a deep sleep.

November was a normally cold month in west Texas. This one would be no different. The storm had blown through from the southwest and brought weather usually driven by a north wind. The temperature dropped to near freezing overnight, and Seth Marlow was not as early as he usually was to open the livery. It was full light as he swung the big double doors wide and stoked a fresh fire in the forge and waited for it to warm the shop. He strapped a heavy leather apron around his middle and sat a blue porcelain coffee pot on the edge of the smoldering coals.

Seth walked around the shop and into the livery to throw hay out for the horses and check on things. One of the horses knickered and looked up.

The blacksmith heard a noise too and picked up a hay rake. "Who's that?" He heard someone stirring in the loft. "Get down here now! I'll shoot if you don't show yoreself!"

"Do not shoot senor! I come down now." Jose was surprised by the blacksmith. He climbed slowly down the ladder and stood with his arms raised high into the air.

"Who are you? What are you doin in my livery?" Seth was more curious than angry.

"I sleep! I no take nothing. I just sleep. Don't shoot me!" Jose was too frightened to see the man did not have a gun.

"I'm not gonna shoot! Put your hands down! Why are you sleepin here? Don't you have a bed?"

"Si senor. I have a bed. It is in Santa Fe!"

"Santa Fe! You come a long way to sleep in my livery." Seth was amused.

"I look for my friend. Ryan Hale. He is my friend."

"Don't know him. He been here long?"

"I don't know he is here. I look for him. He has new son. He need come home."

"Let's drink a cup of coffee, then, we'll go see the sheriff. If he's here, he'll know it."

"Si. I am Jose Gonzales."

"I am Seth Marlow. I'm the blacksmith in Mobeetie. That's the name of this place. Mobeetie."

"Si." Jose had never heard of Mobeetie. "We still in Tejas?"

Seth laughed. "Yep, we still in Tejas! There's talk about changing the name of the town. Some don't like the name Mobeetie. because the Indians said Mobeetie meant Sweetwater, then we found out it means buffalo chip before it dries enough to burn. Town used to be called Hidetown from all them buffalo hunters."

"Si." Jose sipped on the hot coffee. He wanted to go find his friend. He shivered in the morning cold.

Seth found a sign and knocked the dust from it. "You ready to go see the sheriff?" He pulled one of the doors closed and hung the sign on the latch pin. "That'll hold til we get back."

Jose followed the big man down the street and across to the other side. Seth looked through a window and motioned for Jose to come along. They walked into a typical west Texas jailhouse. A two story stone building. it was barren except for a single desk with a rack of rifles hanging behind it. The cells were upstairs

"Howdy John. This here is Jose Gonzales. He's looking for a friend from Santa Fe. Seen anybody new in town? "

"Howdy Seth. Got a stranger upstairs. Don't know his name. Got drunk and busted up the saloon during that storm. Smells like he ain't had a bath in a year. You can look at him if you want to."

"Senor Ryan don't drink. He takes a bath once a week. He don stink." Jose was sure that was not his friend.

"Suit yoreself. Probly not him. Want hurt to look though." John Grayson had been sheriff for many years and seen many things.

He picked up the keys and pointed to the locked door.

"Si, senor. I look. No him, but I look."

The sheriff climbed the steps and opened the door. Jose walked testily into the block of heavy bar covered cells. There was a stench permeating the air as if someone had been violently sick and threw up all over the room. There was the odor of a sun scorched man mingled with the vomit and Jose turned to leave, holding his hand to his mouth. "I come back sometime." He made his way down the stairs and to the front door and stepped out into the cold fresh air, taking a deep breath and filling his lungs.

"That no can be my friend." He turned to Seth as they walked down the boardwalk.

Seth walked along with the young Mexican man in silence. He could see the concern on his face.

"Hey Seth!" It was the sheriff calling to the blacksmith. "That man's horse is still tied at the saloon. You mind boarding it til I turn him loose?"

"I'll do it John. I'll go get him right now." Seth turned to walk across the street. "If you want to wait at the livery, I'll go get this horse. Be right back."

Jose continued to the livery while Seth crossed the street. He entered the stable and warmed himself at the forge while he waited for Seth to return with the animal.

Seth had been detained by friends along the street and did not return right away, leaving Jose to think about what had happened to his friend. His thoughts were interrupted when Seth lead the horse through the open door. Jose was stunned to see the animal that Seth was leading.

"Where you get that Cayuse? That my Cayuse!" Jose had gotten the mount from another livery in Santa Fe, New Mexico.

It was the same one that Ryan had ridden away on and left him stranded in a New Mexico desert.

Both of the men stared at the horse and then looked down the street to the jail. Jose ran through the door and did not stop until he was at the door to the sheriff's office. He stopped for a minute to take deep breaths and then walked in to where the sheriff sat seated at his desk.

"Back already?" John Grayson saw the troubled look on Jose's face and reached for the keys.

The two of them walked to the cellblock with their hands holding a scarf over their nose and mouth. Jose peered into the cell where a man was spread out on a cold, steel platform. It was hard to see what he looked like. He had been sun and wind burned and beaten about the head in a brawl at the saloon. His lips were scabbed and one eye was blackened and swollen

The sheriff opened the cell and Jose slowly approached the sleeping man. Jose had to bend down for a closer look at the almost unrecognizable form on the cot.

He quickly stepped back and stood erect as the man moved and opened his one eye

"Senor Ryan?"

"Jose. What are you doing here? How did you find me? You got a drink? I need a drink."

Chapter Twelve

So he got up and came to his father. But while he was still a long way off, his father saw him and felt compassion for him, and ran and embraced him and kissed him. Luke 15:20

Johnny Warren was looking forward to seeing the place where he had spent his childhood. Anxious about how his father would react at his return, he would not let that stop him from seeing his mother. None of the three men that he rode with knew that his roots were in Coleman, Texas. He had been with Ben Stark since they met near the Palo Duro canyon many months back and had not spoken to him of his home.

Both Johnny and Ben had befriended Ryan Hale along the trail and rode with him in pursuit of Jose Gonzales. Jose had lied at Ryan's trial for the murder of a New Mexico senator and sent him to Yuma prison for two years. Ryan had managed an escape and the three of them tracked Gonzales in an attempt to clear Ryan's name.

When all was said and done Ben and Johnny became close friends and drovers who understood the ways of driving a herd up the trail.

Johnny did not know how he would feel when he saw his Ma and Pa again. He had left home as a fourteen year old and found his way to a ranch in Lincoln County, New Mexico. There he had worked until his boss got involved in the Lincoln County wars.

Johnny Warren had always held life to be a dear thing and did not take to killing other men.

His father had always been a stern man, having very little time for anything but the daily drudgery of trying to survive on a small ranch in the dry, barren lands of Texas.

Johnny's mother was a frail, small woman who loved her man and supported him in whatever he thought was necessary to muck out a living in a hard land. She had spent her entire life within twenty miles of where she lived with her husband and two sons. Her parents, like John Warren, had toiled all of their lives to eke out a living on land that was slow to respond.

When both of them had lost the battle and went to be with the Lord, John Warren had agreed to take her in as his wife. He was not a man that talked about love or showed much emotion or affection but he was kind to her.

Johnny had a younger brother, Kyle, who was only eight when the older brother had had his fill of a man that only knew about hard work. Kyle had watched his brother walk away on shoes that were nearly without soles and a shirt and trousers that were full of holes. The only other thing Johnny had taken with him was a couple of biscuits that his mother had wrapped in a homemade neckerchief of worn denim. He still wore it around his neck as a reminder of where he came from..

Kyle missed his brother and watched their mother cry and mourn for her son when their father was not around. She missed him too.

―――――― ….. ――――――

The four men had ridden out of Clifton, Texas nearly a month before and were all feeling good about saving a house of the Lord. They were headed for Loraine and a visit to the Brown ranch, but before that they were going to Coleman and doing the Lords work once again. They had all prayed together and that was where they were destined to go.

As they neared a town, there were three men on horseback riding at a full gallop behind a single rider. They were coming across the rolling hills east of a place called Brownwood. He was riding hard and gaining ground as he passed them by. Not looking up, he slapped his horse on the rear flank and yelled for him to,

"Come on horse! We gotta go!"

The three pursuers pulled rein as they came even with the four riders. Ben stood in his stirrups and looked down their back trail.

"That hombre must be in a hurry."

One of the riders spat tobacco juice onto the ground.

"You cut a fence, we'll run you outa town too."

" We ain't here to cut nothing mister. We're out to bring folks together." Jonah spoke up.

"Just don't cut no wire. We got a way to fix fence cutters" It was one of the other men, who also spat on the ground and wheeled his horse around.

The other two turned and followed him back toward town.

"What was that all about?" Abe asked. "They looked like they wanted to hang that hombre."

The other three shrugged and they rode at a slow pace until they reached the edge of town. Heads turned and looked at them as if they had committed some kind of crime.

A group of people was gathered around a stagecoach on the right side of the street when they rode in. There was some pointing at two women who were being helped to board the coach. When they were aboard and seated, a cheer went up from the crowd.

One of the women standing near to the crowd spoke in a loud shrill voice. "You go on your way now. You tell all your friends we don't put up with none such as you in this town."

The others who were standing near mumbled in agreement. One of the men spoke. "We don't allow no fence cutters and we don't allow no fancy ladies in this here town."

The four young riders looked at each other and all of them smiled. Jonah spoke.

"I guess the Lord has this town all taken care of. We may as well move on."

They kicked their horses up and rode out the west side of the town. Close by was a marshy looking bayou, which seemed out of place in this country. There were trees lining the banks, and back away from the small body of water. It looked as if someone had planted an orchard. When they had dismounted and walked near the bayou, Ben squatted and picked up a nut that had fallen from one of the trees. He recognized it from his youth in south Mississippi. It was a pecan, and the ground was littered with them. He retrieved another and squeezed them together in his hand til one of them cracked.

"Looks like you know about pecans." Johnny was reminded of his youth in the nearby town of Coleman and the trips he had made to Brownwood with his father. He was beginning to feel nervous about the next few days and what he would do.

———— ….. ————

Four riders entered the small town of Coleman, Texas on a late summer morning. They were on a mission to help the local church. The Lord had directed them to this place. For Johnny Warren it was a trip into the past. He was in awe at the growth that had taken place since he left as a boy. There was no town when he grew up on the small ranch between where the town had been built and a place called Santa Anna Peaks to the south. From the twin peaks, you could see a very long way in all directions. Indians and Texas rangers as well had used the high points as a lookout in times of war. Johnny remembered climbing up onto the peaks to survey his world and to get away from the iron rule of his father's hand.

Coleman was a thriving new town that had a considerable building program in progress. There were six dry goods, one boot shop, one saddle shop, a barbershop, blacksmiths and feed stores and most of all there were three saloons that thrived during the season of cattle drives. Unlike Brownwood, the town's people were glad to see the trail herds that passed along the Western trail and through their town.

The four friends spotted a long hitching rail alongside a long two-story rock building that served as a general store downstairs. The storeowners lived upstairs. They dismounted and went into the mercantile.

As they entered the store there was a hubbub of activity in progress. The storeowner was dumping a large bag of mail out onto the floor and the citizens were digging through it to find their mail.

"What's going on?" Jonah was standing next to the storeowner.

"It's mail day in Coleman. Happens every week. Go to Colorado camp and bring the mail back. It's like a day of celebration. Ya'll must be strangers."

"Yessir we are." Ben answered. "You got any cold milk?"

"No sir, but you can find some over at one of the saloons."

"Thanks." Ben replied and the four of them walked out into the street. It was not hard to find a saloon. The batwing doors and the piano music made them easy to spot.

Johnny hesitated as they began to walk across the street. "I'm going to pass on the milk, boys. I have something I need to do."

The other three stopped and turned to look at him, surprised. "What's more important than a glass of milk?" Abe laughingly asked.

"I never told any of you… My Ma and Pa live out south of town."

All of his friends stood in awe, not knowing what to say.

"I have a younger brother too." Haven't seen them in more than ten years."

"Reckon they got any cold milk?" Ben asked. "We'll go with you."

"I left because me and my Pa couldn't get along. I ought to go by myself, if it's okay. You three can follow later. Its straight south of here. Not hard to find. Look for the Warren place." Johnny threw his leg over the saddle and rode slowly out of town, headed to a confrontation he dreaded.

Jonah, Abe, and Ben, stood in the middle of the street trying to decipher what had just happened.

"I guess we better go get that milk before we ride out." Ben quipped. "I guess he needs a little time." He had known Johnny longer than the other two and was surprised that he had never mentioned his folks.

Kyle Warren looked up from the fence post he was replacing as a rider approached the ranch, raising a cloud of dust. It was a stranger as far as he could tell, but then, everyone who came to the ranch was a stranger. The Warrens were isolated on the small piece of land that they called home, and it was very seldom that someone came to visit.

John Warren was a proud man and accepted no help from any of his neighbors. He felt like people who offered help wanted something in return. He was working in the barn, trying to repair a worn out harness and did not see or hear the coming rider.

Kyle's mother Mattie walked out of the small log house and shaded her eyes with one hand. She had seen the rider coming from the direction of Coleman and was curious to see who may be coming to visit. She had only been to the new town once and her husband John thought it unnecessary to go again.

There was something familiar about the way the man sat the saddle. It reminded her of someone from her past who vowed never to return to this place. She tried to focus on the face of the rider, squinting through dimming vision. Her heart leaped in her chest as she began to realize that her lifelong prayer was about to be answered. It was her Johnny. It was her long lost oldest son. She began to run toward the rider.

Kyle saw his mother start toward the rider and ran quickly to head her off. His mother was becoming frail from the hard life she had been subjected to and the hurt that had been in her heart since Johnny had left those many years ago. He caught up with her and wrapped his arms around her.

"Momma. What's wrong?"

"It's Johnny. My Johnny has come home." Mattie Warren knew who their visitor was. "It's my Johnny!"

John Warren heard a commotion and stepped through the open double doors of the barn. He, for the first time, saw the rider as he drew near to where his wife was standing, being held by their young son. "Mattie! Who is it?"

"It's our son, John! It's our son." Tears flowed down her cheeks.

John's head snapped around to see who was in the saddle. He also recognized the man sitting tall as he rode in. A tear formed in the corners of his eyes. It was his son. He quickly wiped the tear away.

Johnny stopped and dismounted in front of his mother, not even looking in the direction of his father. "Momma. It's me. It's Johnny."

"I know who you are." She pulled loose from her youngest son and stepped haltingly toward her oldest son, not taking her eyes from his face.

John Warren stepped forward and spoke in a cracking voice. "Johnny...." His voice trailed off.

"I didn't know if I was welcome by you. You told me to go and not come back. I just happened to be passing through. I came to see my Ma." Johnny wrapped his arms around his mother.

"Johnny. It's Kyle. Don't you remember me? I'm your brother."

"You're still here Kyle? I didn't expect to see you still around here." Johnny spoke to his younger brother.

"Pa needed help Johnny. You left and Pa needed help."

"I'm different now. I found the Lord. I just came to see Ma." Johnny's voice softened as he turned to his mother.

John Warren turned and walked back to the barn. "I got work to do! If you gonna help while you here, best get to work." It was his way of accepting his son back home. "Help your brother with that fence!"

Johnny ignored his father's comment and walked with his arm around his mother to the log ranch house he had once called home. Mattie rested her head on her son's shoulder, so glad that he was alive and home. Kyle followed along behind them, anxious to hear from his brother what it was like away from the small ranch that he had spent his whole life on.

As the three family members stepped through the door of the house, a thunder of hooves caught Kyle's attention. "More company? We ain't had this many people come by since you left." He directed his comment to Johnny.

Johnny turned and watched his three closest friends ride up to the house. "Howdy ma'am. I hear tell you got some cold milk here." It was Ben jabbing at his young friend.

"Ma, these three are friends of mine. That smart one is Ben. That's Jonah and that's Abe." He pointed to each of them. Get down boys. This is my Ma and my kid brother."

"If I had a Ma looked like you, I would be bragging to everybody. We didn't even know Johnny had a Ma til today." Ben continued the kidding.

"You boys come on in. I do have some cool milk. If there's one thing you have on a ranch, its milk." Mattie laughed for the first time in a long time.

Jonah, Ben, and Abe stepped down and took their hats off and Jonah spoke to Mattie. "Ma'am, you got a fine boy here. He come to know the Lord, and he is learning from the Good Book."

Mattie looked again at her son with admiration. "Come on in. Kyle, you pour these men some milk while I start your daddy's meal. He likes to eat on time."

"Same old Pa. has to have everything done his way." Johnny spoke with scorn in his voice.

"Johnny, don't speak that way about your Pa. He's a hardworking man. Not many men can do what he did to keep this place together." Mattie took up for her husband. "Why don't you go talk to him? He loves you Johnny, and he has hurt for a long time over what happened between him and you."

"Sounds like a good idea to me." Ben chimed in.

"He won't listen to me. He never did." Johnny said.

"He's changed Johnny. You ought to give him a chance." Kyle spoke up. "He's not near how he was when you left. Besides, part of that fight was your fault too."

"He needs your help Johnny. It's getting hard for him and Kyle to keep up with all that needs to be done." His momma had a tear in her eye. She needed him too.

"You leave, I'm going with you. I need to see what's out there too." Kyle was adamant in his tone.

"I can't argue with that Kyle. There is more to this world than this ranch. You need to go see it." Johnny saw the fear in his mother's eyes as he spoke.

"Don't take my youngest son. I was hurting for ten years since you left. Don't take Kyle too!" Mattie did not want to go through that pain again.

"Kyle's a man now Ma. It's time for him to be his own man. He can't keep letting Pa tell him what and how to do everything."

"Pa don't tell me what to do. He lets me do what needs to be done. It ain't like that Johnny. You just had to have your own way. If you found the Lord, you ought to know that." Kyle once again stuck up for his Pa.

Johnny was taken aback by what his Ma and brother were saying to him. Maybe he was wrong. He had been a hotheaded young boy when he left home. He had grown, and finding the Lord was making him begin to rethink what had happened with his Pa and him.

"Why don't we pray about this?" Jonah interjected. Ben and Abe agreed and the three of them knelt and prayed for Johnny and his family. Johnny wrapped his arms around his Ma and brother and listened to the prayers of his friends.

The slamming of the door interrupted them, and when they all turned, they saw John Warren standing, hat in hand, and tears flowing down his face. Johnny walked to his father and placed both arms around his neck. "I'm sorry Pa. I was wrong. Please forgive me."

John Warren slowly brought his arms to encircle his son. He was glad to have his oldest back home.

"I guess we ought to go to town and leave you folks to get acquainted again." Jonah spoke through tears.

"No such thing! You are going to have a meal with us." Mattie was trying to smile through her tears. "Sit!"

Seven people sat at the table and John Warren blessed the food and gave thanks for the return of his prodigal son.

The three friends of Johnny Warren had decided to stay for a while and help get the Warren ranch back on its feet. They had found why the Lord had brought them to Coleman, Texas. It wasn't a church. It was for a family.

The barn was in need of repair and the corral out back was short of a gatepost. Jonah, Ben, and Abe rode out to round up strays and locate as many mavericks as they could find.

The open land around Coleman had not yet seen the fences, as had the neighboring town of Brownwood. John Warren had explained to them that the bigger ranchers were trying to protect the grazing lands from free grazers who passed through on their way to the rails at Abilene, Kansas.

William Day was one of the first trail drivers to come up the Western trail that made its way across the Warren ranch and through the town of Coleman without anyone trying to stop them. Day made it a point to buy mavericks from the local ranchers to increase his herd going north and keep peace along the way.

After a month of working their skills as cowhands, the drovers had swept close to a hundred steers from out of the scrub oaks and mesquite.

They said their goodbyes to the Warrens and began to make their way to Lorraine and the ranch of Aaron and Moses Brown.

Chapter Thirteen

> You shall work six days, but on the seventh day you shall rest; even during plowing time and harvest you shall rest.
> Exodus 34:21

Riding through the town of Sweetwater the three old friends skirted around the stock pens where cattle were being loaded onto rail cars for shipment back east. The cattle ranching business was not doing very well in the drought that the country was seeing. Many ranchers shipped their stock before the extreme dry heat had turned to cold weather, and were taking losses rather than keep and lose them from lack of grazing.

When they had cleared the town on the west side, they found a place to camp along the bank of a trickling river. They were headed to the Brown ranch who were old friends from the days of looking for a promised land. It was only one days ride from where they were camped, and they were looking forward to visiting with their friends.

"Wonder how the Browns are doing in this hot, dry time?" Ben commented as they prepared to build a fire for supper.

"Not good, I think." Abe spoke.

"Can't be good. Those beefs we saw at the rail yard looked pretty scrawny." This time Jonah made the observation. "Them ranchers shipping this time of the year means hard times."

"I sure hope Johnny works it out with his family. He should have told us about them before." Abe was thinking out loud.

"Sure am going to miss Mrs. Warren's good cooking." Ben was thinking about homemade biscuits as he stoked the fire. "Oh well, I know another good cook is waiting for us at the Brown ranch." He remembered Sarah's good biscuits too.

The morning brought a blowing hot layer of rain. All their blankets were wet and the animals looked like mounds of dripping hills looming in the early glow from the east. A bright orange sunlight twinkled through the tree limbs and the wind caused the water to swirl to the ground.

Jonah was the first to roll out of his bedroll and the others watched as he stoked up the fire and started a pot of coffee. Ben threw his blanket back and slowly rolled out onto the wet surface. He shivered in the damp air and looked over at Abe. "You gonna sleep all day?"

Abe grunted and rolled out too.

After the three travelers donned their poncho's and consumed a strong pot of coffee, they mounted and rode off to the west and on to see the friends they had not seen in years. They rode in silence, bundled against the blowing; spinning rain, It was slow going against the wind. All of their horses twitched their heads and constantly blinked against the swirling rain, blinding their vision.

Through the dark gray clouds and the blowing rain, they made their way across a flat barren land. Late in the day as the sun was dropping over the western haze, Jonah led them through the ranch gate and down a narrow lane toward a small log ranch house. Smoke swirled around as it lifted from the chimney. All of them could feel the warmth in their chests as the they neared the long porch spanning across the house.

A man and woman stood near the doorway and watched as they approached, wondering who would be out visiting on a day like this.

"Step down friends. We got hot coffee on de stove." Sarah peered through the haze, trying to make out who had come to call.

"You got Sarah's hot biscuits to go with that coffee?" Jonah removed a kerchief from across his face. "We sure are a hungry bunch."

"Mista Jonah! Do dat be you?" This time Aaron spoke up.

"Howdy Aaron. Howdy Sarah. I do believe ya'll know these two hombres. I found them hanging around San Antonio.

Ben and Abe removed the bandanas from their faces and the two people at the door stared at them, trying to recognize the water covered forms standing at the hitching rail.

"Who dat be mista Jonah? I don't seems to know dem."

"Sad times when a man don't know his friends. Came all the way from Mississippi with the man.... Saved his life and he don't know who we are!" Abe pulled the wet, drooping hat from his head.

"Dat you mista Abe? Dat Mista Ben dere wid you?"

"It's us Aaron. Come all this way in a rain storm just to get some of Sarah's biscuits." Ben answered.

"Come on in dis house outin dat rain. I make you some biscuits to go with dem beans." Sarah laughed and turned to walk into the warm house.

The three riders followed Aaron and Sarah into the warm dry home and into the kitchen that only Jonah had visited before.

"Where are the girls?" Jonah was the first to realize that the daughters of Aaron and Moses were not there.

Aaron and Sarah looked at each other with a sad telling glance. Aaron cleared his throat and turned to his three friends. "Moses two girls done married two Mexican ranchers who live close by. Brothers. Oprah done give birth to a boy child."

"Our girl Ruth done went home to be wid de Lawd." Sarah spoke quietly. "Been five years now.

Kilt by one of them redskins just like her brother. Ya'll member Nathaniel.

None of the three knew that Aaron and Sarah had lost their only remaining child. They all quickly seated themselves at the long table. Sarah moved to the cast iron woodstove and busied herself making the biscuits all her visitors loved.

"Moses, Joshua?" Ben was nearly afraid to ask.

"Dey be out cutting hay for the cattle. Hard times in dis dry, hot weather. We be lucky to have cows left come spring, we don't get some hay for de winter."

"We can help. We got nothing to do right now. Just tell us what you need Aaron."

"Oh no suh, I knows you got bad mens to ketch."

"Not anymore Aaron. We on our way to where ever the Lord wants us to be. Right now, he sent us here to help our friends. You got a bunkhouse we can throw our stuff in."

Aaron looked at his three friends with gratitude in his eyes. "We better eat some dese biscuits and beans. Moses and Joshua be here soon. We get started in the mownin. Po me some dat coffee woman. We gots to get ready to go to work."

———— ..... ————

It rained even more overnight than it had on their journey from Sweetwater. Sarah was up early and had a hot fire going when the men all gathered once again in her kitchen. She bustled about with a new energy. Hot biscuits, eggs, ham and tall pitchers of fresh cool milk lined the table.

The men ate pretty much in silence, after Moses blessed the food. They all knew it would be a hard summer trying to save a herd that was nearly starving if they didn't get some hay put back now. Though the timing was bad, they were truly grateful for the rain...

Joshua had aged well and had become a true cattleman. He had yet to find him a wife. "Ain't got no time to look for a woman." Was his answer when Abe asked. "The Lawd will bring her when it be time." He like his two older brother brothers had found the Lord. and turned into a hard working ranch owner.

Moses went out with his newfound help and, along with the Mexican vaqueros who worked the ranch as cowhands, they loaded hay onto wagons and drove them into the barn where the cattle were bunched in groups, trying to get to the feed. The rain was running in gorges and driving the longhorns to the hilltops. Some were hip-high in the running water and had to be roped and dragged to the high ground.

All the ranchers had learned to harvest the wild grasses in the spring and summer when it was at its peak and stored it in barns to get them through the cold winters. It was harvested by hand with scythes and hoes, and was a long tedious process. Those who had participated saw the fruit of their labors as they saved the hay for the herd.

After a month of working in the hot weather, the rain was beginning to slack off, and the small streams and creeks were settling back into their banks. New shoots of green were showing through the wet ground that only months before had been a drought stricken countryside. Aaron, Moses, and Joshua had survived a drought and a severe summer, thanks to the help of a God sent group of friends.

Jonah, Ben, and Abe were riding to the ranch house, after a long day of rounding up cattle and driving them to another section, when they saw in the distance toward Sweetwater, two riders approaching. They were coming at a slow gait and didn't seem to be in a hurry to get anywhere. It appeared they were coming to the Brown ranch.

The three friends stopped and waited to see who was coming and as they drew closer, Ben recognized one of them.

"That's Johnny Warren. Looks like his kid brother with him. I wonder what's going on." They sat and waited for the riders to catch up with them.

"Howdy Johnny. What brings you out here?" Abe questioned them.

"Long story. Can we get somewhere dry and a cup of coffee?" Johnny had a very troubled look, as did his young brother. They rode in silence until they reached the log ranch house with smoke billowing from the chimney. They all stepped down and knocking the light dampness from their jeans, they climbed the steps to the porch as Sarah walked through the door.

"Come on in dis house. Them Brown brothers already here. I hope ya'll hongry. I see you found some more mouths to eat my biscuits."

"Yes ma'am. This is Johnny and Kyle Warren. They're good friends of ours."

"Dey be welcome. The supper ready to sit to. Ya'll come on."

They followed Sarah through the house to the long table in the kitchen. When they were all seated and Johnny and Kyle were introduced to their host, Moses clasped hands with his brother and each one around the table followed suit. He thanked the Lord for their new friends and the bounty sat before them.

"Let's eat." Joshua pronounced, and they all dug in.

When they were all full, Ben looked at Johnny with a question in his eyes.

"Ma and Pa are dead." Johnny blurted it out and his young brother Kyle wiped a tear from his eyes.

"What! What happened?" Jonah questioned him.

" Pa tried to sell his herd to William Day, who was up from south Texas trying to find cattle for his drive to Abilene next Spring.

"They shot my Pa!" Kyle broke into sobs.

"One of Day's hands said Pa's herd had hoof and mouth. Pa drew on him out of frustration, and the hand shot Pa. It was self-defense." Johnny looked at Kyle as he spoke.

"He still shot my Pa. I would have killed him if you didn't stop me!" Kyle had anger in his voice.

"Your Ma?" Abe asked this time.

"Her heart! When we told her about Pa, she just gave it up. We buried both of them together and the bank took the ranch. Nothing we could do. Word was around about the hoof and mouth and nobody would take any of them. Sheriff came out and we shot all of them."

"You let em. We coulda saved em! We shouldn't have shot em all!" Kyle was still angry.

"What are you going to do now?" Jonah asked.

"Go where ya'll go. Maybe that will get this hate out of Kyle. Where you going and when are you leaving?"

"Another week, I guess. When Aaron and Moses say we're done here. I guess we are going west." Jonah looked at Ben and Abe, who both shook their head in the affirmative.

Moses spoke. "We shore hate to hear about your Ma and Pa. We knows how it feel to lose somebody. Ya'll go whenever you feel. You sho been a blessin to us."

Aaron and Sarah both shook their head. "It been a sho nuff blessin to see old friends. Ya'll needs come back when it ain't rainin and maybe the girls come by." Sarah quipped. "Maybe I learn how to make biscuits by then."

Chapter Fourteen

Otherwise the avenger of blood might pursue the manslayer in the heat of his anger, and overtake him, because the way is long, and take his life, though he was not deserving of death, since he had not hated him previously. Deuteronomy 19:6

Samson Castile Raines reached his twelfth birthday without a mother. The neighbors, Charley and Blue Sparrow Reynolds, had come back home to find the home of their dear friends Samson and Spotted Fawn destroyed by fire and Spotted Fawn buried in a grave under the tree near the Rio Grande River, where she had given birth to her only child.

Cas had a vivid memory of the two men who had shot him and killed his mother and burned her inside their cabin home. His father, Samson had laid her to rest under the tree where Cas was born.

Now that the Reynolds were home and everything was done that could be, he was anxious for him and his Pa to go looking for the two murderers. There had been no reason for them to do what they had, and he would find them and make sure they paid with their life.

Finally, the day came in late spring for his Pa to begin packing a horse with supplies, so they could get started on the trail of the outlaws. He was sure his Pa would not take him along, except that he was the only one that could recognize the two men. He remembered watching a man with a scar over his right eye knock his mother to the ground, while he followed her direction and ran to try to go find his Pa. Another man with a severe limp shot him in the back and when his Pa found him, the cabin had been burned with his mother inside.

There was a mist over the headwaters of the Rio Grande River as father and son mounted and rode away, stopping at a rise to look back at a single small cross under a lone tree near the bank. Near noon on the second day, a place that Cas had only seen twice before. Both times, he had made the trip with his Pa to the way station to sell the few beaver pelts they had managed to trap. This time they also had a few pelts to sell or trade, but they were here for a different reason.

The same old scraggly, stooped shouldered wrangler that Sam and Spotted Fawn had seen on their first stop at the Forks of the river. Sam's thought went back to a run-in with three men on that stop. A man named Tobin had killed one of them and Sam still carried a Henry rifle that had belonged to the dead man. He reached to his scabbard and felt the Henry, thinking of Spotted Fawn as he did.

The station had grown to a small community since that first stop. There were ten or twelve buildings on a street that ran with the curve of the river. They heard a piano clanging from behind swinging doors of a saloon. Samson deposited Cas in the stage station while he went to the saloon and searched for the two men that Cas had described to him. Cas had wanted to go, but understood what his father was doing.

Sam came back and told Cas they were not there and that they would spend one night in one of the upstairs room with beds, and spend the rest of the day wondering the street looking for signs of the two men.

After going in and out of all the stores and other buildings on both sides of the street and searching along the riverbank, Samson took his son into the office of the local sheriff. After describing the two men, they were searching for the sheriff told them the men had been in town for several days and had left after a confrontation with some cattlemen at the stage station. Late in the day as the sun was setting, father and son made their way back to the way station to bed down for the night. The old wrangler recognized Samson from his previous trips to the station.

"Still got that Henry you got off that dead Comanchero?" There was nothing wrong with his memory "Old Kit Carson was here that day. Tom

Tobin shot that one right in the heart. The other two skedaddled out of here real quick like.

"Yeh, that's the two who robbed Charley Reynolds the next day. You seen them since?" Samson was fishing for information. Until now he didn't know who they were.

"They been in and out some. One of em got shot in the leg, and the other one got hit across the head by a redskin with a tomahawk. Almost got him in the eye. Left a big scar"

"When's the last time you seen them?" Samson was really getting curious now. Cas looked at his Pa, waiting for the next comment.

"They just left here three days ago. Headed for the Cimarron strip, I heard em say." The old wrangler did not know the two men had killed Spotted Fawn.

"Better get some sleep. We got to get out early in the morning. We got to get on home." Samson did not want the old man to tell anyone they were trailing the two men."

───────── ….. ─────────

At first light, Samson and Cas were seated at the table drinking hot black coffee and eating flour tortillas and beans with a strip of fatback boiled down crisp. It was a filling meal to keep them for a long day on the trail. Samson had sold what few beaver pelts they had the day before and bought a few more supplies for the trail. The packhorse was already loaded and their mounts were saddled and tied to the hitching rail out front.

Following the downstream flow of the Rio Grande, the two hunters rode slowly out of the settlement and began their quest of the two killers. They were in no hurry to find their quarry, and knew that when they did they would pay for what they had done. For the first time since he was helping his dad track beaver in the mountains, Cas was allowed to carry a firearm full time.

On the second day on the trail, Samson had left Cas at the cook fire while he went to the river to fill the pot for coffee. When he returned Cas was standing very rigid with Samson's Henry pointed at two red men across the fire.

"Don't move. I'll shoot!" Cas was not ready to shoot a man, especially one of his mother's race.

"No need for the rifle son. These are Utes. They won't bother us." Samson turned to the two men. "Neg- tig- a- gand. Friend."

Both of the Indians raised their hands in greeting. Neg-tjg-a-gand. Friend." They sat across the fire, pulled jerky from their pouches, and began to chew the hard, sinewy strips of meat. Cas handed them a flour tortilla and offered them a cup of the hot black liquid his Pa had made in the big blue pot. Both of them shook their head side to side and wrinkled their noses.

"They don't drink coffee son."

"Just like Ma". He said it without thinking.

Samson wanted to know if the red men had seen the men they were trailing, but his Ute was not good enough to communicate. He only remembered a few words that his wife had taught him while they were living next to Charley and Blue Sparrow.

The two Utes stayed just long enough to finish their food and as they had come, they disappeared into the dusk. Samson and Cas curled up by the fire and slept through the night, mindful that they had friends nearby.

There was no way to track the men they were following because they didn't know what they were riding. The only way to find them was asking people they ran into along the trail or listening to others conversations. They heard words here and there that made them sure; they were on the right track.

Samson followed the Rio Grande to the Colorado-New Mexico line and turned east and skirted Ute Mountain, then headed for the Cimarron strip in Oklahoma. It would not be easy to find their prey once they were in the strip. It was known as no man's land for a reason. Only the worst of men made their way into the strip and used it for a hideout from the rest of the world. The Cherokee tribe who had roamed the strip for years had been mostly sent to reservations. There were some free-range ranches throughout the strip, marked only by ranch houses of log and adobe that were mostly hidden under ledges and overhangs near a stream or some sort of surface water.

Samson and Cas made camp that first night in the Oklahoma territory near Black Mesa creek. The creek was running full of clear cold water that had made its way from the Colorado mountains. It made for good drinking water. When they had made a fire and were drinking coffee and eating their beans, tortillas, the sound of horses got their attention, and someone called out. "Hello the camp. I'm coming in."

"Keep your hands where I can see them. Sam answered.

"Don't shoot mister. I'm one man. Lost. Just need directions and a cup of coffee if that's what I smell."

"Like I said. Keep your hands high." Samson reiterated. A man walked slowly into camp leading two horses with his left hand and his right hand high in the air.

"Pull your sidearm and drop it on the ground. Easy like." Samson spoke quietly to Cas, who walked wearily over to the man and picked up his weapon. "Sit mister. Cas, pour the man a cup." Samson kept a close eye on the stranger.

"Mister, I'm a sheriff from over in Mobeetie Texas. If you let me get it, I have a badge in my pocket."

"Reach slow and bring it out. You got a name?"

"I'm John Grayson. Been sheriff in Mobeetie, fifteen years now. I was trailing a man in the strip, but lost his tracks. Kind of got turned around. Got to get back to Texas. The sheriff pulled his badge, passed it to Samson, and took a drink of coffee. "Got anything to go with this coffee. I haven't eaten today."

"How far is it to Mobeetie? " Samson asked.

"A week hard riding, two if you take your time. What are you folks doin out here? "

"Looking for two men who murdered my wife and the boy's mother." Samson read the man as telling the truth and trusted him. "I am Samson

Raines and my son is Samson Castile Raines. His Ma was Spotted Fawn, a Tonkawa maiden."

"Sorry to hear that about your Ma, son. Tell me what these two hombres look like and I'll keep on the lookout for them."

Samson waved his head to Cas, who gave a detailed description of the two killers.

"I'll keep a look out when I get home."

The three men bedded down for a night's sleep, and parted ways after morning coffee. The sheriff headed east to Mobeetie, and the father and son turned north into the Cherokee Strip in search of two men they wanted to bring to their own justice.

Chapter Fifteen

> When you go out to battle against your enemies and see
> horses and chariots and people more numerous than you,
> do not be afraid of them; for the Lord your God, who
> brought you up from the land of Egypt, is with you.
> Deuteronomy 20:1

Crossing into the Cherokee Strip, Samson and Cas rode for two days without seeing another person or animal. They camped on the bank of a narrow slip of water that ran from the northwest to the southeast and cut through a web of arroyos and small shallow canyons. Some places the water dried up to a barren bed that was nearly impossible to find any signs of flow.

Near one of the slow flowing streams, they came upon a log and sod house almost hidden from sight under the overhang in an arroyo. Alongside there was a small corral with two horses munching on dry grass. As they approached, a man stepped from under a hidden entryway. "Hold it. What do you want?"

"Looking for water. Mind if we fill our canteens?" Sam was looking at the man for a scar or a limp. He saw neither.

"Step down and help yourself." He watched as Cas filled the canteens in the shallow stream.

"Raising cattle here?" Sam was making talk as he looked around. For the other horse owner.

"Not many. Mostly free range. Not enough to sell. Mostly feed me and my woman."

"Have you seen two men ride through?"

"Bout a week ago. Two tried to take my woman. Had to shoot one. The other one run off."

"Did one have a scar, and one a limp?" Sam was getting curious. "The one you shot. Did you kill him?"

"No. They both rode off before I could get off another shot. That was the two you described tho. One I shot had a long scar across his right eye. Just nicked him. The other one was limpin back to his horse, and got mounted before I could hit him. Rode off to the north."

"You said it's been a week?" Sam was ready to get after them. "Thanks mister. Your woman okay?"

"They didn't get to her. She'll be alright."

Sam and Cas spurred their mounts and rode away in the direction the rancher had told them. They rode hard for two days, stopping just long enough to get a few hours' sleep. They were not sure how far ahead of them the two owlhoots were, but they intended to dog their trail until they caught up with them.

On the third day before noon, they saw two riders in the distance. It was hard to make out who they were. Sam and Cas slowed their animals and cautiously trailed the two riders. They watched from behind rocks as the prey made camp for the night. They didn't know there was someone on their trail. The pursuers stopped in the rocks and made a cold camp. They ate cold tortillas and beef jerky, while the other two built a fire and made coffee and ate a hot meal.

At daylight, Sam was waiting for the killers to wake. He had made Cas stay with the horses behind the rocks. When one of them stirred, Sam walked into the camp with his Henry pointed at his head. "Stay where you are!"

The other one turned and fired a six-gun and hit Sam in the right shoulder making him drop the Henry. Sam dove to the ground and rolled to one side, grimacing in pain as he rolled on his wounded arm. The man with the scar ran to his horse and was mounted and gone before Sam could retrieve his rifle. The one who shot Sam rolled out of his bedroll and got off another shot as Sam grabbed the Henry and rolled again. This time he got off two rounds and hit the crippled one square in the chest. He turned to see which way the other one had gone and did not see hide nor hair of him.

Sam looked around the camp and touched the dead man with the barrel of the Henry to make sure he was dead. Looking around one more time, he walked back to the rocks where he had left Cas. There was no sign of Cas or his horse.

Near panic, Sam called out for his son. There was no answer. He searched around and finally found two sets of tracks leading away to the west.

Sam searched the area again and then mounted his horse and rode out after the tracks. The wound in his arm was not severe enough to stop him from finding his son. He was riding at a full gallop when he saw the two riders off on the horizon, also riding at full speed. One of them was his son, Cas.

They disappeared over a mound and rode out of sight. Sam kicked his horse in the ribs and tried to gain on the two before they were gone from his view.

He trailed them, sometime in sight and sometime over ridges or behind rocks or in arroyos where he was unsure in which direction they were going. He was worried about Cas and what would happen to him if he didn't catch up with them before dark. His animal was getting tired, but he knew theirs were too. He knew he had to stop, water, and rest his horse. He tried to out wait the man who had his son.

In a deep arroyo, Sam had a flashback to a time when he had been bitten by a sidewinder, and thrown from his horse. That was many years ago and Spotted Fawn, before she was his wife, had saved his life.

His horse began gasping for air and stumbling along the trail, barely able to put one foot in front of the other. Sam knew he would have to stop and rest the horse or lose it.

He pulled rein and dismounted, giving the animal a drink from the canteen that Cas had filled only four days earlier. How long ago that seemed. He thought about how he had felt, losing his wife. He did not want to lose his son too.

Cas knew enough to mark a trail if he possibly could. It would not be easy. The man taking him away would be watching him like a hawk. These kinds of men were devious and trusted no one. Sam knew he would have to keep the pressure on to a point, but not let the outlaw know how close he was. If he saw Sam closing in, he might kill Cas and ride away while Sam looked after his son.

After watering his horse, Sam took a small drink of water. Just enough to wet his throat. He had to save most of it for the animal that would help him save his son. He thought about the anger and hatred Cas would be feeling for the man who had killed his mother. He could only hope that Cas, at his young age, could keep his senses about him. and know that his father was coming.

_____ ….. _____

Cas was waiting while the man who had slipped up on him and knocked him unconscious and tied him to his horse, was now watering the animals. He awakened to find himself thrown across his saddle and riding full-tilt across a country, he did not know. He could only hope that his Pa had found that he had been taken and was in pursuit.

The animals had apparently been rode hard until they could go no more and his captor had stopped to give them water.

"I see you woke up, huh kid. That Pa of yours tries to follow us, I'm gonna cut your throat and leave you for the buzzards to eat. I'm gonna cut you lose so you can sit in the saddle. We can make better time that way. You try anything, you're dead. You understand?"

Cas shook his head, but did not speak. He would wait his chance and the man with him would be the one with the cut throat. Hate and anger boiled up in him when he thought about his mother. He was half-Indian and he knew how to sneak up on a man. His mother's relatives had taught him their ways, and he had learned well.

When the man was watching the trail in front of them, Cas would take quick glances to their back trail. Several times, he thought he had caught a glimpse of his Pa. Never out in the open, but sometime along the edge of a rock formation. His Pa knew the ways of the Indian too.

Because of the horses, they had changed to a much slower gait. Cas's own horse was breathing much better now. He would have to pick his spot, turn his mount to the side, and dart behind a rock before the man in front of him realized it. His Pa would be watching him and would take advantage of any chance to save him or shoot his abductor.

_____ ….. _____

Sam was grateful for the slower pace. It would work to his advantage. He spurred his horse and turned aside making a wide loop around the two riders in front of him, always keeping Cas in sight when he could. The outlaw seemed to think that Sam would not try to rescue the boy. He watched the trail in front of him, but did not check the back trail much. He held the reins to Cas's horse short so there was no way for the boy to reach down and grab them and take control of it.

Sam worked his way slowly closer to the two, until he saw an opening ahead that he could spur his animal through and ride full tilt between his son and the outlaw, snatching up the reins of Cas's horse with one hand and knocking the rider from the saddle with the Henry. He did just that.

Before the man knew what had happened, Sam rode through and knocked him to the ground, drawing his son's horse along behind him.

All Sam wanted at this point was to get his boy away before the man killed him He didn't care what happened to the owl hoot. He would deal with that later. He rode as fast as he could with Cas in tow, and wound them through the rocks and arroyos to get out of gunshot of any lead thrown their way. He was sure the villain would not chase them.

The scarred man would be on his way to somewhere he could hole up and regroup. It would not be to his advantage to follow the mountain man and the kid. He would have to find himself another partner in crime. He felt lucky to be alive. What he needed was a drink and maybe another woman like that squaw mother of the half-breed.

Chapter Sixteen

So your life shall hang in doubt before you; and you will be in dread night and day, and shall have no assurance of your life.
Deuteronomy 28:66

Samson and Cas Raines spent the hot summer months crisscrossing the Cimarron Strip looking for a man with a scar over his right eye. They trailed him from Colorado to the Texas line and back to Colorado again. By early August, they had found themselves nearing Colorado for the third time and Sam was thinking about the San Juan Mountains and his place of solitude at the headwaters of the Rio Grande River.

He and Cas talked about their chances of finding the man they had pursued all summer and how both of them yearned for their home near where Spotted Fawn lay resting. Since they were nearer to home, the two of them decided it was time to give up the chase and go home.

Since the episode with Cas being captured by the scar face, Sam was very particular about keeping his son close by him. He was very watchful and careful of that possibly happening again. He had let his strong desire to catch the two men, put his son in danger. That would not happen again. It dawned on Sam that he had denied Spotted Fawn's strong faith and his own, and he knew it was his responsibility to continue leading their son in the ways of the Lord.

They turned west and found the Rio Grande and retraced the trail that Sam and Spotted Fawn had traveled those many years ago while Cas was still in his mother's womb. Sam found many memories as the made their way along. He recalled their initial siting of the glorious evergreens as he and Spotted Fawn first came to this country.

The Aspens weren't glowing with the golden shimmer yet, but it wouldn't be long. The air was beginning to feel the chill of an oncoming early autumn.

By the end of summer, they had made their way to the settlement at the stage stop at the fork of the river. Cas was seeing things that were familiar to him, and Sam was reliving old memories about his Tonkawa bride.

It was early in the day, so they didn't stop at the river fork, but went on to Wagon-wheel gap. Sam recalled him and Spotted Fawn finding Charley Reynolds after he had been shot and left to die on the bank of the river. Spotted Fawn had used the way of the Tonkawa to nurse him back to the world of the living. That meeting had begun a friendship that had lasted til the present. Sam would be glad to get back to the headwaters and see his friends once more. He and Cas had talked about what they would do and how they would feel upon arriving back to the place where they had laid Spotted Fawn. Cas had suggested they leave the burned ashes of their cabin as a memorial to his mother. Sam agreed. They would build another cabin close by for them to live when the winter snows started. When the weather was suitable, the two of them were happy to sleep out under God's starry skies.

Cas had taken a lot from his mother and the Tonkawa beliefs, except for their pagan rituals. Spotted Fawn had instilled in him that God was real and he must maintain his belief in Jesus. One thing he had gotten from his father was the desire to spend time in solitude.

It was a pleasant time to get back to the Reynolds ranch for both of them. Blue Sparrow's brother Beaver, Pow-inch in their native Ute tongue, even with old eyes had seen them riding along the river and had called out to Charley and his younger sister.

On Sam's first sighting of this place, Charley had called it the Garden of Eden. How close he had been.

Sam spent a short time saying hello's with his friends and then slipped away with his son to visit a mound under the tree near where they would build a new home.

Father and son worked hard in the cool fall days, cutting timber and dragging it down from the San Juan foothills, then, slinging an axe to carve notches for them to interlay into one another, for a tight seal against the winter cold. It was hard, tiring work, but it helped them to sleep at night and clear their minds from the thoughts of mother and wife.

By mid - October they had covered the roof with beams and a heavy thatch. The first fire in the stone fireplace was a welcome feeling against the cold nights. Sam and Cas made a pot of coffee and relaxed for the first time in two months. A necklace and bracelet that Sam had found in the smoldering ashes of their burned cabin, hung from the mantle as a reminder.

On the first morning after the cabin was completed, Charley rode over and had a cup of coffee with the two Raines. After a few minutes of idle conversation, he came to the point of his visit. "Sam, I was down to the forks a few days ago and I heard talk."

"What about?" Sam was curious that Charley heard something that would interest him.

"The man with the scar. There was talk him and two others robbed a bank over in Albuquerque."

"You sure? It could have been another man with a scar." Sam looked at Cas.

They said the scar was long across his right eye."

"It's him Pa! It's got to be him!" Cas interrupted. "We got to go Pa! We got to go find him!"

We will go see if it's him. We will go this one time. If it's not him, we will forget about him. Agreed!" Sam looked straight into his son's eyes.

"Okay Pa. If it's not him, we come home to stay."

"Charley, we will leave tomorrow morning, so we can be there before the snow gets to deep. We will go across the San Juan's to Durango and cut across into New Mexico"

"I'll look out for the place til you get back home, Sam," Charley spoke quietly. "Try to make it in time to see the spring flowers. Scarlet Paintbrushes come early."

———— ….. ————

Seth Marlow had been thinking about finding help to take care of the livery part of his shop. He was a blacksmith and didn't think much of mucking out horse stalls. Jose Gonzales had dropped into his hayloft as if by miracle. Seth offered him a job for a place to sleep and food for him and his friend, Ryan Hale. Jose had been overjoyed and thankful for a place to try to bring his friend back to the Lord. and away from that demon in the bottle.

Ryan had been raised in the home of a preacher and had never tasted alcohol in his life. When he had lost his wife, he turned his back on God and had lost himself in the bottle. His mind was fogged and the booze was the only thing that would take away the pain of losing his only true love. In the daytime, he hung around the saloons, begging drinks or sweeping the floor for whatever he could get. He had become a source of entertainment for the steady crowd.

When the saloon had closed or whenever Ryan was passed out from the devil in the bottle, Jose would carry him to the livery and lay him gently on the hay bed he kept for him. Seth Marlow was a Christian man and was very understanding of what Jose was trying to do.

Jose spent his days cleaning stalls and helping Seth in whatever he needed done. When he had to drag Ryan out of the saloons; Seth would allow him to take care of his friend.

Ryan was unrecognizable after two months of drinking and not taking food into his body. He had not shaved nor bathed since he left Santa Fe.

The weather was extremely cold and the snow covered the countryside all that winter and there were few visitors to Mobeetie

_____ ….. _____

John Grayson had gotten back to Mobeetie a few days after meeting the mountain man and his son near the Cimarron strip. He had kept his word and checked around, looking for any sign of the scarred man and one with a limp. He was unaware that Sam Raines had shot and killed the gimpy one in the strip.

Word came to him in early October that a scarred man and two others had robbed a bank over in Albuquerque, New Mexico, not too far west of Mobeetie.

John had become friends with the young Mexican man who Seth Marlow had given a job at the livery. The young, hard-working peon was totally dedicated to helping his friend get out of the bottle. Jose had confided in John and Seth about his years of being right where Ryan now was. He and Seth had watched many evenings as Jose hauled Ryan to the stable and tried to get him to put food into his body.

In early December, when the snow was falling in two-day blizzards and the saloon business was down to almost nothing, Ryan was having a hard time finding drinks. He would spend his days hanging around, hoping some straggler would come in and buy him a drink. Jose would not help him in his search.

Seth and John made a suggestion to Jose on one of the hard falling snow days as they were warming around the forge in the blacksmith shop.
Seth was the first one to bring it up.

"Jose, I know a way we can help your friend dry that liquor out of his system. That is… If John here will go along?"

"What do you have in mind Seth?" The sheriff was curious. So was Jose.

"Well, you could lock him up til he gets sober and over the shakes." Seth said.

"On what charge, Seth?"

"Don't need one. He's too drunk to know. If Jose goes along, we can get him sobered up."

"Si! Senor John. We can do that. I think that will do. We get him out of the bottle, I read the Bible to him, where he cannot get away. Si!" Jose was excited about getting his friend sober.

Samson and Cas rode across New Mexico and into Albuquerque in a blinding snow storm. They made their way down a long, winding street that followed along the Rio Grande River and searched for an office with a light in the window. When they had found one, Sam stepped down and walked to the door. After he was sure, it was the sheriff's office he waved for Cas to come in out of the cold. They walked into a room warmed by a large pot-bellied stove and saw and elderly man seated behind a desk. Cas went to the stove and held out his cold hands.

"Cold night to be out stranger. Can I help you with something?" The man looked at Sam suspiciously.

"Looking for three men. Heard they robbed a bank here. One had a scar. Here" Sam raised his hand and pointed to his right eyebrow.

"That they did. Got away with it. Killed one of my deputies. What you got to do with it?"

The one with the scar. He murdered my wife." Sam spoke as he looked at Cas, warming himself by the stove.

"Don't know what to tell you mister. Last, I heard they was headed east. If they get to Mobeetie, Texas John Grayson will probably lock them up. He's the sheriff there. Real good lawman." The sheriff mentioned a name that Sam had heard before. "You better find a place to get out of this weather. Hotel ought to have plenty of rooms. If you don't mind you both can sleep here. I don't think I'll have any more guests tonight."

"That'll be good sheriff. I don't think my son has ever been in jail." It was the first warm place they had been in days. Sam and Cas both were used to sleeping out in the cold. Sam thought about the time he and Spotted Fawn had been to Albuquerque. They had stopped at the San Felipe de Neri Mission, looking for a couple who would take two children they had found in the desert.

The sheriff left and closed the door behind him, closing the father and son in the Albuquerque lockup.

He was back early the following morning and made a pot of coffee for them. A young woman came in with a tray piled high with biscuits and side back.

The snow had stopped for now and after a hearty breakfast Sam and Cas said their farewell and rode east across New Mexico and on toward Mobeetie Texas.

Chapter Seventeen

For I was hungry, and you gave Me something to eat; I was thirsty and you gave Me something to drink; I was a stranger, and you invited Me in; Matthew 25:35

Jonah, Ben, Abe, and now Johnny Warren and his young brother Kyle rode away from the Brown ranch and headed west. They did not know where their next stop was to be. They would pray along the way and wait for the Lord to give them a direction. There was not much in this part of west Texas except barren desert land. They had stayed with the Browns until late in the summer, helping them to get the ranch back on its feet.

On the third day, they crossed over a large spring that dumped into a small gorge between the base of a scenic mountain and a neighboring hill to the southwest. They filled their canteens with the cool sparkling water and allowed their horses to drink their fill.

All of them decided to rest for a few days and pray about where they were to go from here. They would ask the Lord to guide them. While they relaxed and walked their animals through the cool spring waters, they saw two men riding from the south. Both of them were wearing the blue trousers of a Calvary uniform.

The two riders rode into their camp at the spring. "Howdy strangers. Going to Santa Angela?" The older of the two asked. He looked a timeworn army sergeant who was old enough and ready to retire.

The younger man had nothing to say.

"What's in Santa Angela?" Abe was the one who asked.

"Not much, less you lookin for whisky and women. Fort Concho is there to protect them from the Injuns that ain't. Mostly that's where them ladies get their money, from them soldiers."

"Ha! The women don't get much from them soldiers. Most of em is buffalo soldiers. You know what is buffalo soldiers, mister? They is black boys, left over from fightin in that big war. Most of em is freed slaves."

"Don't mind him gents. He's goin to Fort Worth to hang. He killed one of them women. I'm just his escort. I'll be back at Concho fore long. Got six more months til I retire. Them I'm goin to Californy to see that blue water."

"Is there any more white soldiers besides you? Kyle asked the sarge.

"Not too many, but a few. We could use a few more. You want to join the army?"

Alright if I read to him from the Good Book?" Johnny interrupted. He wanted to try to see if the man was a Christian and get Kyle's mind off the army...

"I don't care if he don't." The sarge didn't put much stock in the Book.

Johnny spoke to the sarge. "Got a church at that town? "

"Got a chapel at the fort. Nobody uses it much. Don't think I seen a church." The old soldier was not too enthused.

I'll tie this hombre to a tree and be out of your way, come mornin." He turned and walked his and his prisoner's horse to a pinion tree at the edge of the spring.

The soldiers were gone at first light and Ben was the one who started the coffee pot.

"Know anything about the army, Ben?" Kyle walked to the fire behind Ben.

"I know that war is not a good thing. Killing people is a hard thing. I don't know about killing Indians. Can't be any different from that big war. Killing is killing."

When Jonah and the others got out of their bedrolls, they all gathered around the fire and listened to the soft sound of spring water tumbling into the gorge. Jonah was the first to speak. "Anyone feel the pull of the Lord?"

"I thought it might just be me. I woke up knowing that is where I must be." Johnny Warren looked at his brother as he spoke. He was holding his Bible open in his hand.

"We gonna stay there Johnny?" Kyle read something in his brother's eyes.

"We'll have to wait and see... I think this is where the Lord want's us, but we'll see."

"If you think this is it Johnny, we'll help you get started." Jonah knew what was happening, and so did the others in the group.

They all quietly saddled and mounted their broncs and rode south along the North Concho River and into whatever the Lord had in store for them.

——————— ····· ———————

Riding along the river, for two days, they saw on the horizon, a high wall fort. Marching around the outer perimeter were soldiers in close order drill. The only white man among them was a tall, lanky sergeant, barking out commands. He yelled at them at every turn, trying to keep them in a straight formation. Kyle watched with intense concentration as they rode by. Each one of them carried a rifle on their shoulder making sure they were all in a straight line.

They rode into a town that was lined on both sides with saloons, brothels, and gambling halls. Men staggered from one to the other, most not knowing where or what they were doing. It didn't matter to them as long as they had the money in their jeans to participate in the fun. The five riders continued until they had passed all the way through the raucous town.

On the far end of the street, separated from the activities were a small one-room schoolhouse and an even smaller building with a steeple. Both were in need of paint and repair. The church door was hanging loosely from its hinges. Johnny stopped in front of the building and dismounted. He looked at his friends and shrugged his shoulders. All of them stepped down and walked into the church. The pews were in place and only needed dusting. There was a small podium up front.

Johnny walked slowly up the aisle between the pews. He had his Bible in his hand at his side. He had never even talked to anyone in public, but he was being guided and was unafraid.

"Ya'll gonna starts a church?" They all turned to see who had entered the door behind them.

Two black women stood at the door. "Ya'll gonna starts a church?" One of them asked again. "We be wives of dem buffalo soldiers over at de fort. We sho does need a church."

Kyle walked down the aisle. "How do you get to be one of them soldiers?"

"You not de right color to be one dem buffalo soldiers. You gots to be black. You can be one of dem white boy soldiers if yo mammy let you. You looks kind of wet hind the ears." She smiled at the other woman. "Ya'll sho nuf gonna starts a church? We sho do needs a preacher in dis town. One of you boy's a preacher?"

"We are all men of God. Don't know how good we preach." Jonah spoke softly.

"Praise de lawd!" The other woman spoke up." The two women left to go spread the word.

―――――― ..... ――――――

For the next week, the men of God pitched in and rebuilt the little church. One of the black women brought six more volunteers over to help. She also showed Johnny a small house only two doors down that served as a home for the preacher.

Kyle disappeared one day and was gone for several hours. When he showed up again, he was wearing the blue uniform of a Calvary private.

He was proud to be a man and old enough to serve his country. Johnny was happy for his brother and glad that he would at least be able to stay close. At least for a while. Jonah, Ben, and Abe stayed around for two Sundays to hear their friend bring a sermon to the residents. Not all of them were from the fort. Some of the businessmen were guided by their wives, and surprisingly some of the saloon girls showed up.

Chapter Eighteen

Let your light shine before men in such a way that they may see your good works, and glorify your father who is in heaven. Matthew 5:16

Jonah, Ben, and Abe had gotten Johnny settled in at San Angela and knew he was the right man in the right place to serve his God. His small congregation was already growing with the wives from the fort bringing along their soldier husbands.

It was time to be on their way to the north and back to Palo Dura Canyon where their friend Charles Goodnight had begun building a ranch. They were not sure where the Lord was directing them, but it seemed like the right way.

They traveled along the Concho River, retracing their way to the springs where they rested before... Moving along, they rode for another week and stopped at the yellow canyon where the Lubbock post office was located in a strange looking building that was painted yellow to match the canyon walls. The post office was in poor condition and seemed to be deserted. There were no signs of water.

The three riders bedded down out behind the building and left at daybreak. There was not much between the yellow canyon and the larger canyon at Palo Dura. Dry brown grass covered the land that they rode across. The weather was beginning to get colder and the clouds had the ominous look of a snowstorm.

When they had made their way to the rim of the Palo Dura canyon, the snow was beginning to lay a sheet of white across the grassy desert. Down below they could see small herds of cattle at different places on the canyon floor. Near the Red river, they could see a small structure that Charles Goodnight used for a ranch house. They inched their way down into the deep canyon and found their way to the ranch house.

Charles Goodnight greeted them and was glad to see them back. Ben and Abe had both worked for Goodnight on trial drives from Texas to New Mexico and Colorado.

WINDS OF AR-MAH-REE-YUH

——————— ..... ———————

Jonah had never felt out of place with his cowhand friends before now. He had not driven cattle before like his two compadres except those few weeks at the Brown ranch.. He had listened to them talk about cows, chuck wagons, and trail drives for a week. Charles Goodnight was the first rancher ever to put a box on the rear of a wagon for the cookie to store his wares.

He heard Mrs. Goodnight speak several times to her husband about saving the few buffalo that were about to disappear from the great western plain. Buffalo hunters from the canyon to Hidetown had slaughtered thousands of the animals for their hides. Hidetown had changed its name to Mobeetie, after most of the buffalo were gone.

When Ben and Abe had decided to come back and work for the Goodnight ranch, Jonah made a decision to make his way to Mobeetie to the northeast. All of them had heard tales of the rough town of buffalo hunters, buffalo soldiers, and cowhands that inhabited the many saloons and bawdy houses in the town named after buffalo chips.

As in Santa Angela, a fort housed buffalo soldiers. Fort Cantonment had been built to protect settlers and hunters from the Indians. The fort as well as the town had changed its name to Fort Elliot.

That is where Jonah felt the Lord calling him. Ben and Abe thought they must go along with Jonah to Mobeetie and see what was there.

The three friends rode out the northwest end of the canyon and circled around to the direction of Mobeetie. Along the trail, they spotted lone shaggy brown buffalos. Once, they saw Molly Goodnight instructing cowhands to bring the lone buffalo calves to suckle at cows on the range. The cowboys didn't look any too happy.

Ben and Abe looked back and waved at their friends, then turned their attention to the cold ride.

It was a cold snowy day when they rode into the wide-open town. Huge signs proclaimed the business that was prevalent in Mobeetie.

There was The Pink Pussycat Paradise, The Buffalo Chip Mint and The White Elephant. Two miles from town was the Ring Town Saloon that was primarily for the black buffalo soldiers. They rode down the main street and like in Santa Angela, the schoolhouse and church were located at the outside edge of town and both were in need of repair. The friends dismounted and walked inside the church and knelt at the altar and prayed together. This was where the Lord had been leading Jonah Caleb Smith since he had come to the Promised Land.

They walked out into the street and went into the schoolhouse, and found a desk with one leg broken off and a blackboard hanging from one corner. When they stepped outside a man was standing in the street.

"Can I help you with something?"

"Maybe. You got a school teacher or a preacher in this town." Jonah spoke up.

"No sir, but we could use both. You a preacher?" The man looked from one to the other.

"We are all men of God. Who are you?"

"I am Seth Marlow. I own the livery over there." He pointed over his shoulder to a livery across the street. "You planning on staying?"

"I'm Jonah Smith. This is Ben Starks and Abe Tobias. Glad to meet you mister Marlow." They all shook hands with the stranger. "Looks like a really rowdy town".

"Buffalo hunters are starting to leave. Soldiers not too bad. They pretty much stay to themselves. Bars are going to go broke. Be a nice town before long." Seth smiled. "I know a few ladies who would be glad to help you clean up. I don't know about a teacher."

Three days later, Seth had sent six women over to help with the cleanup. They were happy to serve and looked forward to having a church service and maybe a school for their kids.

———— ….. ————

Two men came riding into Mobeetie just at sunset. They rode to the hitching rail at one of the busy saloons and stepped down. Stretching their legs and arms, they looked around, walked up the two steps to the boardwalk, and crossed over to the swinging doors. Loud piano music blared into the cool evening air.

They looked around cautiously and stepped to the long bar. The bartender looked up and stared into the face of a man with a long, jagged scar over his right eye. "Whiskey!" The barman continued to stare at the man.

"You see something you don't like?"

"No sir!"

"Pour me another. Got a lawdog in this town?" He scowled.

"Yessir. Down the street on the other side. Want me to go get him?" The barman was looking for a way out.

"Let sleeping dogs lie, I always said. I'll get around to him in my time. Got any squaw women in this here town?"

"Yessir. Down the street near the end of town. Breeds and blacks down there."

The scarface slammed his glass onto the bar, turned and walked to the door, followed by his cohort, who had not spoken a word.

Jonah and Ben had been working with three of the black ladies, cleaning the schoolhouse and getting it ready for the new school year. They had not yet found a teacher, but were hopeful.

When they came out of the door, two men walked down the street, leading their horses. When they saw the women, they stopped and stared in their direction.

Jonah and Ben looked at each other and turned to the ladies. "Thank you ladies. See you tomorrow."
"Hold it. I didn't say you could go!"

"I did!" Jonah loosed the flap on the hammer of his revolver.

The man with the scar reached for his six-shooter and cleared leather. Before he could get off a shot, another revolver got off three shots. One hit the scar face in the heart, and the other two downed his partner. Neither Ben nor Jonah had fired.

The sheriff of Mobeetie had fired and dropped the two outlaws. He walked over and turned them with his foot. "Bartender told me they were here. They are wanted in New Mexico for bank robbery." The women scurried down the street to their homes, fear on their faces.

"I'm John Grayson, Seth told me you were cleaning up the church and school. I'm the sheriff in Mobeetie. Which one of you is Jonah Smith?"

Jonah stuck out his hand. "I am. Do I know you?"

"No sir, but I've heard of you. You used to be Marshall in San Antonio?"

"Yessir, I was. I'm in the service of the Lord now. I plan on being the preacher in this church."

"Well, good luck. I guess I better go do the paper on these two. Got to send a telegram to Samson Raines and tell him that one is dead." He pointed to the scar faced body.

"Who!" The three said in unison.

"Samson Raines. That one killed his wife."

"Samson Raines from Colorado?" Jonah spoke this time. "We all came to Texas with him. When did it happen?"

"Back in the spring. I ran into him and his son in the Cimarron strip looking for that one." He pointed to the body again.

"Son?" They all had a questioning look on their faces.

"How long has it been since you seen him?" Grayson asked.

"Twelve years or so I guess. We didn't know his wife. We heard he got married. Didn't know he had a son. How old is he?"

"Looked to be about twelve." Grayson answered.

Chapter Nineteen

And He did not let him, but he said to him, " Go home to your people and report to them what great things the Lord has done for you, and how He had mercy on you." Mark 5:19

Sam and Cas rode into Mobeetie, Texas expecting to catch up with the man who had killed their wife and mother. Sam scanned down the street lined with saloons, looking for the office of Marshall John Grayson; He saw an office on the right next to what appeared to be a newspaper office.

They turned in and dismounted, tying their horses to the rail. Both were tired and cold from a long hard ride. It had snowed on them nearly all the way from the Texas line and they had slept out in it. They had crossed the north edge of the Palo Duro canyon and saw the deep drifts down the sides.

When they walked in the door, Sam saw John Grayson seated behind a desk and over to one side was a set of stairs. The office was cold and felt like a dungeon, not much warmer than the outside. The walls were made of thick stone.

"Sam! I just sent you a telegram yesterday. What are you doing here?"

"That scar robbed a bank in Albuquerque and headed this way. I'm on his trail. You see anything of him?"

"Sam. He's dead. I killed him yesterday. Him and one of his cohorts."

"How?"

"He was about to get into a gunfight with three men who just came into town. I think you might know them. They know you."

"Who? How. I've never been here."

"One of them is the new preacher. Name is Jonah Smith."

"Jonah! A preacher? Last I heard he was a Marshall in Bandera."

"Two others with him. Ben Stark and Abe Tobias."

"Ben and Abe?"

"That's what they said."

"Where are they?"

"I spect they're down at the church. Cross the street."

The front door to the jail opened and a young Mexican man hurried through and closed the door quickly behind him. "Hello, senior John. I not know you are busy. I come back."

"No, it's okay Jose. These men are about to leave. Sam, this is Jose Gonzales. He has a friend upstairs. Jose this is Sam and his son Cas. They are new in town. Go on up. Ryan has gotten much better. He is about back to normal."

"Si senor. Glad to meet you senor. Glad to meet you too." He acknowledged Cas and walked toward the stairs.

"Come on Sam. I'll show you where the church is." John got up and led Sam and Cas out the door. Cas had heard his Pa talk about his friends that came to Texas with him. He knew that Sam would be glad to see them.

They strolled down the street through the icy crust of snow and crunched their way to the small church. There was the sound of voices, singing; Rock of Ages, emanating from inside. Sam, Cas, and the sheriff stayed on the porch until the singing had stopped. There were women and men raising their voices to the Lord.

Sam instructed Cas on what to say and the youngster stepped quietly inside the door and stopped with his hat in his hand. "Anybody know where I can find a preacher? My Pa needs a preacher bad."

"Where is your Pa, son? Is he hurt?"

"No sir. He just needs a preacher. He said he would like one from Mississippi. Does that help?"

The three veterans flashed back to a time at the end of the civil war when they had met in a swamp.

Ben asked. "Who is your Pa, son?"

Sam stepped through the door. "He's right here."

"Sam!" All three of them exclaimed, as they rushed to the door.

Cas and the sheriff stepped back and allowed the old friends to enjoy their reunion.

"What made you become a preacher?" Sam enquired of Jonah.

"The Lord!"

"What about you two?" He turned to Ben and Abe.

"We going to be drovers forever for the Lord. That's what he wants."

———————— ….. ————————

All of the warriors were back together for the first time in over twelve years. They spent many hours reminiscing about the times they had coming to the Promised Land.

Cas was in awe at the stories that the four of them told. The congregation put together a Christmas program that had all the children involved. Cas was talked into playing one of the three wise men.

On the third Sunday, Jose was allowed by the sheriff to bring Ryan to the service. He had started eating food again, and had not had a drink in weeks… It was to be the first time that Ryan had encountered the Lord outside of the prayer time with Jose and Seth Marlow in his cell.

Jose had found that Ben Stark was in town helping the new preacher with the church and he came and prayed with them.

Ryan remembered the times they had spent on the trail together searching for Jose. It was good to have someone from Ryan's past to help.

They walked to the church and got there just before the service was to start. Jose opened the door and held it, watching for Ryan's reaction as he entered. Ryan seated himself on the back pew and listened intently as Jonah Smith preached about the return of the prodigal son.

When the service was over, he was the first to leave, shaking as he walked into the cold January weather. He held onto Jose's arm and spoke to his friend. "Jose, I need to go and see my son."

Jose did not speak, but was so happy in his heart that his friend was thinking about his son for the first time since the death of his wife.

As they stood on the street having the conversation, Jose saw a look of disbelief come across Ryan's face. "It can't be." Ryan whispered under his breath. "It's a miracle."

Jose turned to look at what Ryan had seen. All he saw were the four friends who had gotten together for the first time in years. Jose recognized one of them as Ben Stark, the man who had helped Ryan track him down, but Ryan knew who he was.

"Samson! Samson? Is that you Samson?"

Sam Raines turned and looked at the young man calling his name. "Yes, I'm Samson Raines. Do I know you?"

"I'm Ryan, Samson, Ryan Hale. Don't you remember me? from New Mexico. Me and my sister Sissy."

"Ryan, Ryan Hale. It can't be. What are you doing here boy? Where is your sister?"

Ryan looked at Jose. "She is in Santa Fe with my son."

"You have a son? So do I! This is my son Cas." Sam introduced Cas to Ryan.

"My son is half Mexican and Indian too." For the first time Ryan was proud to be a father. When I get home, I'm going to give him a name. Samson, Benjamin, Jose, Hale."

_____ ….. _____

The winter began giving way to a typical west Texas spring, and all of the compadres had spent many hours together renewing old friendships and cultivating new ones Cas had made many new friends through his fathers and the other warrior's tales of the past. Ryan had told Samson all about the time he had spent in Yuma prison for a murder he did not commit. Jonah, Ben, and Abe had talked about a young man named Johnny Warren, who Ryan had also met during his quest of true freedom from the prison.

All of them had suffered losses in their time in the Promised Land, but all of them had made it through with the help of their Lord.

The snow had melted and Sam and Cas were thinking about the cabin that was waiting for them in the Colorado Mountains. Sam wanted to be there when the spring flowers peeked through the last snow.

Ryan and Jose were thinking about Santa Fe, New Mexico, and Ryan's young son. They had sent a wire to Ryan's parents, informing them that he had returned to God and that he was coming to take care of his son.

Ben and Abe were yearning to get back on the trail as ranch hands.

Jonah had found his calling and was spending time with his Lord and learning how to lead his sheep.

One of the saloon girl's had previously been a schoolteacher and through Jonah had come back to the Lord and to the children.

———————— ..... ————————

One early spring morning, Ryan and Jose boarded a stagecoach for Santa Fe. Sam, Cas , Ben , and Abe mounted their horses and rode alongside. Two days later, they crossed over the north end of the Palo Duro Canyon. Ben and Abe were near to where they would once again be trailing cattle for Charles Goodnight.

There were yellow flowers sprouting all over the countryside.

Ryan Hale whispered quietly under his breath. "Ar-Mah-Ree-yuh."

They were all going to once more, renew their Winds of Freedom.

Find this and other books by this author at…
Booksbyguy.com

Winds of Freedom
Winds of the Rio Grande
Santa Fe Sundown
Winds of Ar-Mah-Ree-yuh

Made in the USA
Charleston, SC
10 June 2013